THE CHOSEN PENGUIN

by

Warren O'Hara

CHAPTER 1: FOUNDATIONS OF AN EMPEROR

The Emperor penguin was an inventive species, a great engineer when compared to the rest. No one else cared for building or measuring like the Emperor penguin did. It could be said without hyperbole that the Emperor penguins were always thinking of how better to make their environments. After all, they were the ones who lived in the harshest of climates. They were the ones who spent long periods of the year, particularly the males, in the stormy interior of Antarctica huddled together for warmth, clinging to life in a bitter world.

#

Like so many penguin species, a great many Emperors, who called themselves *Greenies*, believed in *The Greenmaker*. Of course, He was not known to other species as The Greenmaker. For the Gentoo, for example, he was known as *The Redmaker*. And the Chinstraps for their part called him simply *Light Bird*. Whatever were his name, it was He who shone down on all of them on certain nights of the year with much fanfare of colour and play, the green curtain of light, sometimes red, streaming across the sky, mesmerizing all the upturned beaks that took in its beauty and metaphorical warmth.

If there was a bounty of food from the sea and the weather was somewhat bearable, it was put down by the Greenies to be that of The Greenmaker up there somewhere being content and generous. If, however, food was in short supply and a blizzard pelted the faces that tried to turn away from its lashings, it was presumed that for some reason or other The Greenmaker was angry and vengeful. To appease Him, all Greenies would huddle together not just for corporal heat and to build social cohesion but to sing and squawk in praise and in humility to The Greenmaker: for it was He and He alone who hath given life; and it was only He who would take away that same life.

And when disagreeable things happened there on Antarctica, disagreeable things such as famine or a rogue leopard seal killing several members of their colony, one of the Greenie clerics would raise a solitary flipper into the air and say: *The Greenmaker worketh in mysterious ways*. And all there would nod their heads solemnly and agree, and would bray out that agreement, the collective sound sonorous and pleasing in the cold air: for who amongst them or any other of the colonies out there could rightfully know the workings of His mind, the mind of The Greenmaker?! And though they could not know His mind, they could at least offer Him their unconditional love and loyalty and ever-willing signs of appeasement, lest they be next to be engulfed by the jaws of death.

In time, one of the Greenies whilst diving had happened upon a green gemstone near the seafloor. It was a beautiful stone and did not lose its glint when taken out of the water and dried. This stone was quickly incorporated into the Greenie Order and became sacred, thereafter aptly being called *The Sacred Greenstone*. Whatever the occasion in Greenie circles, The Greenstone was at the heart of it: for they believed this to be a part of The Greenmaker, a physical manifestation of Him down here on the ice.

#

And through millions of years of evolution, through untold seasons of surviving in a barren ice world, the Emperors were able to become resourceful, efficient, intelligent and hard-working. Therefore, it came to them gradually that they should stack up a wall of ice and snow so as to cancel out the ferocity of the katabatic winds. And that is exactly what they did time after time after time. Wherever Emperor penguins amassed, they would first erect a high wall of snow and ice, a windbreaker, so as to be able to keep warm all the better.

And so, since the wind's direction was likely to change by season or even to change over and over again on a single blustery day, the Emperors easily took to the task of erecting four walls instead of one. And naturally enough, it did not take them long after that to realize that they could be even warmer between the four walls and sheltered from the snowfall if they could lay down a roof above all. And, despite much protestation from Greenie zealots who considered a roof as sacrilege, as being that which would sever them from Him up there in the night sky, that is exactly what came to pass too.

And in no time their buildings became smaller and more circular. In a word, their dwellings became igloos. And these igloos were built to measure, built to be the warmest edifices they could be. Yes, most of these igloos were just large enough to accommodate a standard family.

Henceforth, the penguins would be as snug as a bug in their abodes, both Mama and Papa, both Chick A from last season and Chick B from this season, and if there was a bit more room, there was even a place for Granny and Gramps. Yes, having shelter from the elements at last was one less thing for the Emperors to worry about. The first of many less things as well.

#

Many, many seasons passed, and ever inquisitive, the Emperor penguins were soon able to create and fashion a totally raw phenomenon of nature, namely, fire. By gathering driftwood from the ocean and the blubber from dead seals and beached whales, the penguins were able to set up their pyres. And then, by using a thin layer of ice as a lens when the sun was shining, they were able to set alight the whole shebang. And these fires were kept smouldering for weeks and months at a time since it was unknown when the sun would next shine, and in their wintertime down there in Antarctica the sun might not make an appearance at all – and if it did, it would be so wan so as to be unable to spark anything into flames.

By trial and error and since they had not yet stumbled upon the concept of chimneys, it was quickly grasped that fires lit inside igloos led to lungs being choked in smoke. Furthermore, indoor fires inevitably led to melted roofs caving in and smothering the hapless residents who would have to dig their way out of the little avalanche with their flippers. Of course, some never made it out alive. And so in those pre-chimney days, fires had to be prepared outside, sometimes protected by three high rudimentary walls of ice and snow somewhat off at a distance in order not to melt said walls and at the same time to keep the wind and blizzards from quenching out the fires.

And so, fire really was a game changer in Antarctica. Although, it must be said that initially the Greenies, who were somewhat highly strung and of a fundamentalist disposition, considered fire, as they had one time considered roofs, to be sacrilege, an imitation of The Greenmaker and His performance in the night sky. These Greenies would not partake either in the gathering of fuel or the lighting thereof. They preferred to stand half-frozen far away from the flickering flames or in their igloos and to shiver the day and night through in moral superiority.

But it could be noticed over time that these same zealots stood a little closer to the fires. It turned out that moral superiority could only ever last so long when one had been shivering whilst convenience had been radiating out at a stone's throw. And once the penguin shivering deemed the shivering itself to be needless, it was the end of any semblance of demonstration, was the ceding of any moral high ground. Yes, the zealots would eventually come around to fire, would eventually join the majority around its glow and there tell stories of yore, or debate over fish and squid and the best places to catch them, or debate over the growing numbers of a certain seal colony or the dwindling numbers of another.

And now, the zealots, instead of railing against fire, regarded it as a gift from The Greenmaker, its flames a gift in His image. And the fact that fire would now be used to incubate the Emperor penguins' eggs was another sure sign that The Greenmaker, giver and taker of life, was giving them the means to accelerate the stage of the unhatched to that of hatchling.

In truth, fire was a massive benefit. No longer did the males have to waddle about or stand stock-still out in the cold with an egg tucked beneath a layer of skin above their feet. No longer did the males have to do this until the eggs hatched. No. Quite simply, a fire could be lit when possible to do so or flames were taken from a smouldering one in the middle of the colony, and while the eggs were kept warm beside it, kept from freezing solid, the parents collectively could concentrate their efforts on other things, such as hunting for food or repairing any damage the winds had recently wrought upon their igloos. Yes, with fire came more free time. Much more free time.

#

And like all tools that fall into the flippers of those who can wield them effectively, nothing would ever be the same again. The ceremony of watching the sky for the presence of The Greenmaker was still kept by the Greenies; however, when The Greenmaker was absent, all Emperor penguins stared not at the sky and its many stars but at the flames that lit up the familiar faces all around. To be sure, they would gather around the large public fires and squawk loudly and stare into those flames that moved about hypnotically. And they would rejoice from the light and the heat.

Verily did many Greenies feel blessed and favoured by The Greenmaker for having fire. Many would rejoice from the thought that He had gifted them a piece of the sky, its wavering not green but, like the markings on their plumage around the topmost breast, orange. Some Greenies, however, staring at the same fire as their fellow-congregants, would think themselves in fact to be the ones who were godlike: for in their minds it was they who had made fire and not He; it was they who had stoked a ballet of flames into life. Yes, they would think to themselves, *it was not He who had created this but we.*

#

In no time at all, with their ever creative minds, the Emperors were able to construct fireplaces and chimneys in every single home. Now for the first time ever, penguins were able to manipulate the temperature, albeit in a small area consistent with the size of their abode and done so as to ensure the igloo walls would not melt, or at least would not melt too much thereby. And the effects of this piece of ingenuity were massive. Especially from a social perspective. The large huddles of the entire colony became a thing of the past except for when meetings needed to be convoked. Families, although interacting in the acquisition of food and the repairing of the few necessary waddleways that crisscrossed the colony, could now keep to themselves at night.

Although social cohesion was not damaged too much by each igloo having its own fire, families did seem more prone than before to squabble over the most trifling matter. Only the Greenies kept up the lighting of public fires and huddled together around them in praise of the The Greenmaker or ventured outside of the colony merely to watch Him in his purest state, exhibiting his display in the sky.

And it was around this time that the inevitable schism occurred in the Greenie circle: those who believed themselves creators of fire in lieu of The Greenmaker, those who had begun considering themselves godlike, now broke away cleanly from the Greenie Order and began calling themselves Penguanitarians. Now what a Penguanitarian was and what a Penguanitarian believed in were two things that were still very much unknown by the others, and perhaps even by the Penguanitarians themselves. But what Penguanitarians did not believe in was known to all and expressed to all, rather frequently at that, especially to the Greenies.

#

It was not long after the discovery of fire and its benefits that the Emperors thought up of another way to improve the living conditions for their clan. And that was the idea of nets. Sure, penguins still swam in the sea and hunted their prey there. But what about at night? When nightfall fell on Antarctica and The Greenmaker played about with His curtain of green light, the penguins could not fish. If only there was a way for them to be able to fish at night too – that would ensure they take in double the amount of food. But even if they *could* fish at night, that would entail double the work, and that would also mean that penguins would have no rest time whatsoever.

And then it happened. Then a new invention came onto the scene. Another game changer. The Emperors devised nets. Simple toboggan-of-the-mill nets. At first, they were small nets and caught only prey that offered half a morsel. But in time, the Emperors could fashion huge industrial-sized nets that would cover large swathes of the sea and be left there overnight beneath the ice. Of course, the hard part of it was breaking the ice, which could be very thick indeed. And almost always, especially in wintertime, and if the netter did not have a spare net with which to do the old switcharoo, the ice had to be broken a great deal for setting the nets and broken yet again when hauling them up.

But for all that hard work, the next morning there would be enough food in a few large nets to feed a colony of penguins for an entire week. Therefore, with more nets, with tightly-meshed nets for small prey and loosely-meshed nets for large prey, the penguins eventually had no need at all to swim in the frozen seas in search of food, neither by day nor by night, no need to swim the gauntlet of leopard seals and orcas, no need to die needlessly for a beakful of krill. No, now they did not have to go to the food: the food more or less came to them, and, what's more, it came to them when they were sleeping.

#

And so, having constructed shelters that kept one out of the wind, having cradled that oh-so-wondrous fire, having engineered nets that could feed entire colonies over and over again, and having even created storage facilities for food as a sort of future investment, just in case there would be days, weeks or months of shortage in the ocean, or in case their nets would be destroyed by whales, the Emperor penguins went about furthering the availability of free time, improving the living conditions for their subspecies.

And once their subspecies was thriving, once the Emperors had huge gulfs of free time due to their technological innovations, it did not take long for them to consider the plight of their brethren, the other penguin species who still laboured out in the open, the other species who still lived in a barbaric state. To be sure, if The Greenmaker had shone so kindly upon them, thought the Greenies, perhaps they themselves should not be so selfish and should therefore share both their faith and their modern conveniences throughout the region. And this was a concept that the Penguanitarians were quick to seize upon and whittle down to make their own.

#

Penguanitarianism, they called it. And it was a warm and fuzzy ideology. It began sluggishly, making very small inroads into the minds of all Emperor penguins except for the most zealous Greenies and The Elders of Instinct, the latter a group of old penguins who believed in tradition and the natural order over anything they deemed abstract.

Penguanitarianism was a belief system in which the Emperor was meant to forgo all interest in his own colony in order to put himself in the webbed feet of all penguins, regardless of their species. The idea was that one was to waddle around in constant guilt for having the warmth of a fire and a roof over one's head and a limitless food supply. One was to constantly think of those other penguins somewhere out there who were iglooless in this cold world. One was to think of those whose stomachs were empty. One was to think of the frozen eggs laid waste to by the howling winds, embedded there as a stark reminder in the snow and ice, never to crack open and spring into new life.

Yes, the Emperor penguins now had the time and convenience thereof to think of all this, and to think of all that was beyond their colony, of which they knew nothing if anything.

#

A penguin in the colony who mended broken flippers and such, and was known simply as the *bodybird,* a kind of sage as it were, of whom it was said knew a little about a hell of a lot, was often asked by the rest why other colonies from other penguin species, the Adélies for example, did not have the great things and the large gulfs of free time that they themselves had. And the bodybird, a quiet fellow, would say that different species had different overall ways of looking at the world. And what might be good for one species might be poisonous for another. And therefore, all species should stick to their own and not worry too much about things that are far removed from their own environments. And then he would conclude with the refrain that had become a tiresome cliché for them:

Birds of a feather flock together.

Of course, for stating things that, the bodybird was often berated and ridiculed; but being a cheerful penguin, he did not take any of this to heart and would nod his head and waddle off to his business.

No, the Penguanitarians and Greenies thought, their universal beliefs merging somewhat, *it is nothing to do with differences in species since a penguin is a penguin withal. It is not cold empirical facts but Love that wins the day.*

And the Penguanitarians themselves brooded further on the topic:

If it is not His Love, then it is a penguane love amongst all penguins of the world – a love to better the living conditions for all and thereby reign in a feathership utopia. For once an egg is nurtured and once the chick is nurtured thereafter, the adult penguin, whatever be his or her species, will be as law-abiding and as assiduous in the daily chores of colony life as your average Emperor. And even if the penguin be old, and even though The Elders of Instinct say that you can't teach an old penguin new tricks, the Love of Nurture or, as those silly Greenie's claim, The Greenmaker's love, will still convert the old fellow into a model citizen, into as able a worker as the young Emperors who dig through the layers of ice so as to set and haul out their fishing nets. Yes, whether hitherto he or she had dabbled in a little bit of the chick-killing and cannibalism, that same he or she will be exactly the same as your average Emperor when guided by a nurturing flipper. If the noble savage does not appear noble to us, it can only be due to his not having opened up his heart to the heart-warming principles of Penguanitarianism. Yes, all is possible if only one just believes. All is good if one only refrains from being prejudiced for once and believes that all are *good. Nurture. Not genetics. Nurture over Nature forever and ever and ever. All it takes is patience and love,* the Penguanitarians would chant together around the fire. *All it takes is patience and love. Patience and love for one's fellow-penguin.*

To be sure, the Greenies had had many a conference on the topic of sharing His love to the poor savage penguins who did not know what they were savages. And yet again did they reach that conclusion after much braying that if The Greenmaker, who maketh life and destroyeth life, had gifted them all the material comforts, it was only right that they share His love and bounty to those other penguins the world over and thereby make the world a better place. And perhaps, some of the Greenies thought, that by sharing both faith in Him and in His technology, The Greenmaker would make a special place for them in the sky. A kind of quid pro quo. Serve Him, spread His message of Greenliness and be rewarded with eternal bliss up there in the night sky. Yes, when they would squawk their final squawk, He might turn *them* into a star, as He had done for many of their ancestors long ago. And if they shared His gifts to all penguins, maybe he would make them the biggest and brightest star in the night sky, twinkling ever brighter when caressed by His green curtain of light.

#

Anyway, development in the Emperor colonies came thick and fast. Their ingenuity and solutions to all sorts of problems seemed to know no bounds. Both hatcheries and nurseries were set up.

Hatcheries were essentially large buildings with huge fireplaces where hundreds and hundreds of eggs were tended to by three broody old females. For The Elders of Instinct the hatchery was their crowning achievement: for by it was the propagation of their subspecies both accelerated and increased.

The nurseries were more or less schools, non-mandatory, wherein little chicks were taught how to be good citizens; how to be good chicks and to show respect to their parents; how to love their tribe, their subspecies, its history, its traditions and its exciting plans for the future; and, of recent note, much to the dismay of many of The Elders of Instinct, who felt their power and influence waning in the colony, encroaching ever more into the nursery curriculum was how to accept the universal precepts of Penguanitarianism, and Greenliness too.

#

A vital component of the education system too, but which was somewhat in decline, was that of swimming. Early on, when less and less penguins were taking to the water, when swimming was no longer essential for survival, it was decided amongst The Elders of Instinct that it should still play a key part in what a penguin was.

The Elders of Instinct, though the decision-making process for the entire colony was slipping further and further away from their flippers, declared over and over again at meetings to anyone who would listen that an Emperor penguin who could not swim, or who did not want to swim, was no longer an Emperor penguin: for if one disconnected oneself entirely from the sea, one would be something else, a different creature altogether.

CHAPTER 2: THE STRANGER & THE SIX CHICKS

It was a day like any other when the horizon was broken by six tiny silhouettes. And as the silhouettes enlarged, as they drew ever closer, those Emperors with the sharpest eyes could note by the waddling, that the silhouettes were penguins too. But the sharp eyes could also note that the waddle was not that of an Emperor penguin. And then another silhouette appeared on the horizon too. And this one seemed to catch up quickly with the other six. And this one was much taller than the others.

      Twenty minutes was how long it took these newcomers to reach the Emperor penguin colony. And quickly, the newcomers could be identified not on penguanal terms but as a related subspecies given the brighter orange plumage on the sole adult's head, and breast, and there was even a splash of orange on his beak too. The six chicks, unlike the black and white and grey plumage of Emperors, were brown feathery fluff balls. Yes, all were identified as being the long-lost cousins of the Emperors. These newcomers were six King penguin chicks and one very, very old King penguin male. All seven of them were gaunt and shivering. All seven of them had been ravaged by a blizzard or a score thereof. And all seven of them were woebegone to look at, had even the pallor of death upon them, though the old male's black beady eyes sparkled with some hidden source of vitality. None of them either brayed or squawked. It was not known if they were able to speak the Emperors' language or if it was due to their poor physical condition, the long beaks, the longest of all penguins, being frozen, perhaps even frozen shut.

Of course, this event was like squid from heaven for the Greenies, but more so still for those adherents of Penguanitarianism, particularly for the females: that a number of poor and starving penguins from not just another colony but from a completely different subspecies, albeit deemed to be, genetically speaking, a closely related one, should come into their midst in need, in desperate need, was like a drug for them, a kind of euphoria. And they quickly surrounded the newcomers, fussed over them and led them to shelters wherein blazing fires were in operation. There they swaddled them in wearable nests of downy feathers and served them regurgitated food and freshwater. And the six King penguin chicks, of which three were male and three were female, and who it was discovered were the offspring of the Old King that had brought them here, rested their weary heads on the chests of six partially prostrate, chickless Emperor penguin females.

And the Old King penguin himself paced the floor of the igloo that been provided for him. And after much of this pacing, he then stood by the blazing fire to thaw himself out. And no sooner had he defrosted himself than he lifted the flab of skin that was above his feet to reveal a large chunk of silver. He clasped this piece of silver to his orange chest and lay down with his back to the doorway. Then he made sounds, sounds that told any other penguins within earshot that the Old King was finally fast asleep.

CHAPTER 3: PENGUANITARIANISM RISES

Much was now astir in the colony. It was as if the inevitable had finally come true. As if a great giant had finally awoken from its slumber and there was suddenly much to do. Indeed, there was no time to waste for the Emperors: a decision had to be made that very night. Should the King penguins be sent packing in the morning? Or should they be allowed to stay indefinitely?

It was arranged and all attended, even those hermits who rarely ventured out of their igloos, especially at such a bewitching hour. Indeed, the meeting was arranged. The Elders of Instinct and a few Penguanitarians chaired it around one of the central fires. There was much to discuss, even though a great many Penguanitarians and Greenies already believed that there was nothing to discuss at all apart from trying to bring in more suffering King penguins and, while they were at it, to bring in Chinstraps and Gentoo and Adélies as well, to bring in any moving thing so as to show the guests what constituted the generosity of The Greenmaker or the Love of penguane Nurture itself.

All were called to order and the excited squawking and braying died down. To be sure, the Elders of Instinct would bring to the fore of this meeting the subject of instinct, instinct and little else to guide them in what they considered was for the colony's welfare and future. And they declared with much curtness now that they would offer their opinion, and that that opinion would be based for the most part on instinct: for it was instinct that had served the colony well thus far and it was instinct that should continue to serve it going forward. And their instinct told them that these newcomers, notwithstanding their poor physical condition and plight, were, to put it succinctly, no more than harbingers of doom. Large sections of the audience became angry on hearing this.

    The Elders of Instinct continued speaking their minds through raucous boos and squawks. And the more resentful became the crowd, the more The Elders of Instinct spoke undeterred. Even if it was going to take them twice or thrice as long to get their point across in such a hostile audience as this, get it through they would. And even though the female Emperors bewailed their words and screamed at how the poor King chicks would perish if they weren't allowed to stay, The Elders of instinct nonetheless explained how taking in these seven newcomers was one thing, but that more would come in their wake, that many, many more would come in time; that the word would get out that there was a free lunch to be had in the Emperor penguins' territories. They explained too about how as other species' populations would swell here in their advanced colonies in just a few decades hence, there would be, indubitably, horrendous civil strife and war. Such was nature, they said, that one subspecies would try to outcompete another. Such was nature that one subspecies would try to annihilate another and that that was why Penguanitarianism was fish pie in the sky, a belief system with no credibility in the world. They stated that nowhere was it present in nature, nowhere at all, where subspecies could interact in the same ecosystem and yet remain intact at the same time, either both disappearing through hybridization or the more dominant subspecies ending up enslaving the other and thereby bringing about its extinction or even haphazardly that of both. The old refrain *Birds of a feather flock together* had not lasted the test of time for no reason, they said.

    Exclamations and execrations rose further amongst the

crowd, even among the Penguanitarians that were chairing the meeting with the Elders of Instinct, who bethought themselves no better opportunity in their lives than this to challenge the Ancient Order, to play to the gallery and score political points. Nevertheless, the Elders of Instinct spoke more, putting forward all the information they had at their disposal on the King penguin too.

They spoke about that species at length. Indeed, they had heard their forefathers speak of that type of penguin, and not in the most endearing terms either. Legend had it that the Emperor and King penguin long ago were one and the same, but how something happened very fast and suddenly there was a huge chasm between the two.

The earliest legend, a sort of genesis, touched upon the notion of a primordial soup whose surface was tranquil until a meteorite struck it and thereby brought the surface to ripple, which consequently brought a single cell into life beneath the surface. And from this single cell were good and evil. And good and evil could not reside in the same entity. Both migrated to their own side of the cell and tugged with all their might. And the cell was sundered. The good cell, which was the bigger one, became the Emperor penguin. And the evil cell, which was the smaller one, became the King penguin. And ever after, the King penguin wanted to destroy the Emperor penguin and rule supreme over every facet of nature.

Another legend claimed that all birds, both flying ones and the flightless, were descended from reptiles. And it was said that unlike all other birds whose brains had developed with that metamorphosis over eons, the King penguin, birdlike though he was to all intents and purposes, had not developed the birdbrain. In fact, his was still the reptilian brain, a brain bereft of compassion for anyone or anything apart from himself. And with that reptilian brain of his, there was never a moral dilemma or a sleepless night over making a decision. No. It was said that a King penguin never made a single decision because he just was and he just did. Ipso facto, he had the autonomy of a virus. He was merely the finest specimen or manifestation of the parasitical spirit, a spirit that was ever present and at the forefront of nature.

The Elders of Instinct then regaled the screaming crowd with the story of two penguin brothers, one kind and hardworking, the other mean and lazy, the former he who would become the sire to all Emperor penguins, the latter he who would become the sire to all King penguins.

Another legend bespoke an Antarctic glacier as large as a ten thousand colonies, on which were many penguins. The glacier snapped off and fell into the sea, thereby becoming an iceberg. After many months at sea, this iceberg finally made landfall on the coast of Argentina or Chile, subsequently leaving the future King penguins to their fate on a foreign landmass and developing into a different subspecies completely.

Some legends claimed that a geographical barrier had separated the original tribe in Antarctica, a mountain or such, and over time they developed into separate tribes, developed as separate subspecies, the King penguins becoming troublesome and pernicious to the Emperor penguins when that barrier was no longer impossible to transcend, and who thereafter were expelled from the continent by the Emperor penguins who could no longer afford to have such a nefarious subspecies as their neighbours, let alone on the same massive continent.

Other legends pointed to the branching off between the two tribes as to being due to climatic conditions, Antarctica originally being a warmer place, and how the Emperor penguins which were today taller than the Kings and three times as heavy, were much better adapted to this freezing climate than were the Kings, who as a consequence of the Big Freeze eons ago had to migrate to South America and some of the sub-Antarctic islands, which were less cold.

More recent legends stated that the separation between the cousins had been brought about by a *krillino* (gene) for trickery and deception, a mutant krillino coming about in the ancient penguin population, and how its further replication since it was advantageous to have in that environment back then, evolutionarily-speaking, had led to the Emperors realizing that their own survival was dependent upon them banishing the carriers of that gene of trickery, namely, the King penguins, from Antarctica for once and for all.

Of course, there were manifold legends, rarely told nowadays around the fires and with the night being short could not be regaled now, especially with so many penguins beginning to flap their flippers in the air with agitation. But even though they were not brought up now, The Elders of Instinct did think about them as they faced off the outraged Greenies and Penguanitarians. And some of these legends mentioned the King penguins coming back to Antarctica time after time, and always coming as tricksters, as downtrodden and grieving victims of some injustice perpetrated by the Chinstrap or the Macaroni or the Gentoo, and claiming kinship through blood and their sharing common krillinos with the Emperor penguins, and in no time these King penguin visitors would drive the Emperor penguin colony into anarchy, bloodshed and despair.

One legend in particular related a whale carcass being gifted by the Kings to the Emperors. And the Emperors, thinking this a kind gesture from their cousins, took in the carcass and left it in their camp overnight. However, within the carcass were to be found some two-thousand bloodthirsty Adélies, who cut their way through the carcass with their beaks and went about surrounding and massacring the entire colony of Emperors, who at that time had been dozing on their feet in a huddle and had no way to escape the onslaught..

With their lectures on legends and old stories at a close, The Elders of Instinct claimed as calmly as they could muster in the feverish throng of Greenies and Penguanitarians that the King penguin was a dangerous penguin. Of course, he was their brethren – that could not be doubted. Yes, he was one of the penguins that was most related to him the Emperor. But he was a different creature. Not so much physically apart from size of course but by his modus vivendi. The King penguin, The Elders of Instinct would announce in what was now a cauldron of reproach from the crowd, was a user, a cheat; he was not a builder of societies, rather he was a demolisher thereof whilst at the same time feathering his own nest thereby.

And such claims as these by these Elders of Instinct led to something that had never happened before in living memory in any Emperor penguin colony: The Elders of Instinct who had spoken thus were first spat on by the crowd and then given an almighty pecking, all amidst such execrations as *blasphemers, sinners* and *penguin-haters*. When one of The Elders of Instinct tried to bring up another of the plethora of legends that denoted the never-ending war and famine that were ever present with the King penguins, his words were guffawed. *Legends!* the crowd chanted. *We've had enough of your tired old legends. We came here to a meeting to find out what measures would be taken to safeguard our new residents and this old superstitious fool wants to regale us with more silly old legends. Made-up stories is what they are. Stories for hatchlings and nothing more. And we wouldn't even tell such penguin-hating stories to a newly laid egg lest such bigotry seep in through the shell and corrupt the developing mind of the chick.* And when that Elder of Instinct persisted and began to mention the Legend of the Whale Carcass, he was immediately set upon and even had one of his eyes pecked out, which gruesomely hung from its socket until the tendon holding it finally snapped and the unblinking eyeball fell into the snow and was trampled underfoot by one of the angry protestors.

Furthermore, some members in the crowd levelled the accusations at these Elders of Instinct that it was they who were the demolishers, how it was they who wished to stop progress and revert the clan back to the ways of old, when eggs were regularly frozen into eternal death, and when starvation and blizzard-exposure were ever present factors. And so, bleeding and bruised, The Elders of Instinct were further beaten by the crowd that was now a baying mob. And this baying mob pushed them and jostled them and finally ejected them from the meeting.

Thus were The Elders of Instinct left far away from the

central fire and left languishing out on the cold outskirts of the colony. And this was no mere symbolism: The Elders of Instinct, those who had spoken out against accommodating the King penguins indefinitely, were really to be left out in the cold forever more. No longer would they be allowed to warm themselves at any fire in this Emperor penguin colony. No longer would they inhabit any igloo there. No longer would they be afforded the right to eat any of the fish caught in the industrial-sized nets or dispensed from the storage facility, which was now called the Food Wareigloo. No, henceforth, they were to live their lives out there in the blizzards, where icicles would hang and glitter from their very beaks. Yes, and being old, they would not have the physical ability to found a new colony either.

And now, with The Elders of Instinct gone, their monogamous partners gone with them, it was presumed that they would all perish. But, either way, The Elders of Instinct were no more and were quickly forgotten about. And excitedly, feverishly, the Greenies and Penguanitarians looked forward to a new dawn in colony life, a new way of doing things, which included opening up all they had to the rest of the world and thereby making the rest of the world all the better for it.

And thus that night was it decided, by way of a landslide too, Penguanitarians and Greenies forming what would become known hereafter as The Council, each member thereof rubbing his flippers with glee or backslapping another member, now with the power of carte blanche, that the King penguins could stay…indefinitely. A great cheer went up from the crowd. And, not only was that decided, but it was decided too that all penguins, wherever they came from in the world, could come to their colony: for there was no limit to either physical space or quantity of food once penguane Love of Nurture or The Greenmaker's Greenliness reigned supreme, once Penguanitarianism or His generosity was taken into the hearts of all penguins. That was what all agreed upon then and there as they dispersed from the meeting, their spirits as high as the green curtain of light that played silently across the night sky.

CHAPTER 4: THE OLD KING'S SPEECH

The King penguin chicks stayed with their new adopted mothers while the Old King penguin, a thick layer of nesting now around his neck like a shawl, waddled his way slowly the next day to the central fire to relay to all and sundry the harrowing experiences which he penguanally had witnessed in Tierra del Fuego. And to say that the Old King had a captive audience would be a gross understatement: all of the Emperor penguins, but particularly the females, hung and gushed on his every word.

The Old King was an able speaker. Many were surprised to listen to him speak the Emperor language almost as fluently as any native. He could even sprinkle his speech with some colourful slang which fused well with his overall formal style of speaking. And boy could this King get in many a word into his sentences! Had he not been interrupted on several occasions, he could easily have spoken from sunrise to sunset, have spoken and still kept up an interesting and vivid account of his miserable life and of his suffering tribe, a tribe which seemed to be the perennial victims no matter where they went in the world and no matter with whom they tried to reach out to befriend, and all because the King penguins believed that all penguins should be given the benefit of the doubt, no matter their species or subspecies..

And thence would the Old King highlight what barbarity could be enacted by those other species. Momentarily ruffling the Penguanitarians' and Greenies' feathers there, he spoke of the bloodthirsty Gentoo who had invaded his penguins' colony and slain sixty percent thereof, amongst whom had been his very own doting wife.

Now, some there knew a little about King penguins, and they knew that a female could only in general rear two chicks within a period of three years; however, the Old King had claimed after having just arrived at the colony that all his chicks, some being older than others, were all from his union with his wife. The numbers and times of course just did not stack up. And that could only mean that the Old King had been lying. That could only mean that if all six were his chicks that they had come from several unions. And that would mean that the Old King was not as monogamous a penguin as he claimed to have been. But taking all this into account, and having witnessed the vicious attacks on and the expulsions of The Elders of Instinct, no penguin dared to raise this conclusion publicly.

Anyhow, for all that, the Old King spoke of the Macaroni penguins too, who were, according to him, a devious bunch of penguins, who had double-crossed time and time again the poor hapless King penguins, so many times in fact that they lost much of their territory to them and had to end up living on ice floes, even in stormy seasons, and how thereby many of the King penguins had been hurled into the sea by waves bigger than mountains, and, if not drowning there and then, were first harangued in a despicable game by schools of orca who, dwarfing the King penguin, would make a sport of torturing him, throwing him hither and thither until finally getting bored and gobbling him up whole.

And to everyone's delight, particularly to those hardcore Penguanitarians and Greenie zealots who had cringed when the Old King had spoken ill of the other penguin species, of whom he had painted a very grim picture indeed, he immediately and cleverly brought the oration back around to their liking. Yes, the Old King informed the Emperor penguins that despite being double-crossed by the Macaroni a million times, and despite being almost exterminated by the Gentoo, all King penguins still held to a sacred belief that all penguins, no matter the background, could be saved from barbarity, and saved from needless suffering too. And to both astonish all and to further delight the eager Penguanitarian listeners, the Old King announced that all King penguins believed wholeheartedly in a philosophy, and that philosophy's name was...Penguanitarianism.

Now a large section of the crowd cheered in unison. A huge welt of joy went up into the sky. But how on ice could a different subspecies whose colony was far, far away from theirs reach the exact same reasoning!? How indeed! A few wondered about this. A few wondered if the Old King had been within earshot of or had snuck close to the previous night's meeting and had copied the idea from what he'd heard being said in order to pretend now that he was right in with a large part of the colony's way of thinking. Yes, some thought that and studied the Old King's features, especially those bright beady eyes that contrasted with the haggard face and beak. Some thought that he had earwigged and copied what he'd heard. They did. But they knew it to be unwise to share such a thought with others in case they too would end up like The Elders of Instinct, who were now nowhere to be seen, not even a few miles from the outskirts. For all that, though, most of the penguins believed what they wanted to believe: that Penguanitarianism and its precepts were universal; that Penguanitarianism and its precepts were independent of any single subspecies or species of penguin because it was a creed, a love that engulfed all without exception.

When the cheers had died down, the Old King resumed speaking. His visage took on a glummer expression now. Oft times throughout this latest part of his oration, the Emperors clapped and clapped. and cheered and cheered, but the Old King would raise his flipper each time in order to communicate to the crowd that now was not the time for jubilation: now was the time to listen, to listen, because he had some vital information to share with them, more vital than anything of which he had hitherto told them. And then, as he got to the business part of his presentation, a sudden crack of emotion entered the old King's voice. An emotion that had not been there heretofore.

And what the old King revealed in his emotional voice was a pleading. A pleading to save the small remnants of his tribe who were stranded on an island that was full of leopard seals. He said he understood that to rescue his beloved tribe would be no easy task, but that Penguanitarianism meant saving all penguins who found themselves in peril no matter what the subspecies or even species. And all he would be able to offer the Emperors if they would be so kind and penguane in varying out this one task, in sending out a number of their finest to rescue the remnants of his tribe – and he put serious emphasis on the word *remnants* – well, all he would be able to recompense them with for such a penguane act would be that of love, love and loyalty, a loyalty that would never be broken, never! And with that final statement, the female penguins immediately surrounded him and embraced him, some of which even swooned and had to be dragged off to their igloos. And for those females who clung and embraced the Old King, it was only with violence that the male penguins could pull them off him and stop them from crushing his decrepit little body to feathery pulp.

And so it was agreed unanimously. As unanimously as had they voted on letting the Old King and the six chicks stay in their colony. Yes, on the morrow the Emperors would set forth and undertake the arduous journey to that island that was full of those dangerous and snarling beasts called leopard seals. And by hook or by crook, they would bring back the few King penguins that remained, which, according to the old King, were not the last King penguins solely on that island but the last remnants of the great tribe that existed in the entire world. Yes, the Emperor penguins would save the King penguins from extinction, even though in reality the King penguins were more plentiful than ever, were even more plentiful than the Emperors themselves. But of course, the Emperors, dripping with emotion and holding out their flippers to each other around the public fire so as to connect and feel the warm fuzzy mushiness of Penguanitarianism, knew nothing about the world outside of Antarctica these days. Since they had invented igloos and discovered how to harness fire and how to fashion nets that caught fish while they slept, they knew nothing at all about the goings on in the outer world. And the Penguanitarians and the few Greenies who now tobogganed The Council, before adjourning the meeting altogether, asked if any of the community would like to ask a question, or if they had any grievances they would like to air, or if there were any suggestions they would like to offer so as to make the Old King and his six chicks feel more welcome in the colony.

Now there was one young penguin in the crowd that day who was deeply troubled. Although he himself believed without a shadow of a doubt in Penguanitarianism, he felt there was a certain inconsistency therein that just had to be addressed. And when the chance was given for plebe penguins like him to speak or air any grievances they might have, this young penguin swallowed hard, mustered up all his courage since hitherto he had never spoken publicly at one of these meetings, and raised a solitary flipper. Suddenly those who were standing around him moved a little away so that all could see the better who was about to speak. All beaks turned towards him. All eyes were now on him. In particular, the young penguin noticed that the bright beady eyes of the Old King were set on him with much intensity. Nevertheless, the young penguin rasped his throat and spoke softly. But alas, his voice was too soft and many at the back of the crowd could not hear what he was saying. And so, the young penguin raised his voice as much as he could. It turned out that he had a question for The Council and the question would toboggan into a whole host of questions, all of which were about Penguanitarianism.

He asked the Penguanitarians in The Council if the tenets of Penguanitarianism were such that all penguins, no matter their age or species or subspecies, could be converted into model citizens and believers in the greatness of Penguanitarianism. The Penguanitarians in The Council grinned wryly. What a redundant question! The female penguins blushed and cooed. Such an innocent and beautiful question from such a young penguin, and so mannerly in the way he asked it too! Yes, the Penguanitarians in The Council responded with joviality and a sort of firmness. Yes, Penguanitarianism was universal; therefore it could be taken up by any penguin species or subspecies anywhere in the world, whether young or old. And the young penguin nodded while the Penguanitarians were responding to him, and when their response had ended he continued into his next question: *if a penguin so happens to sin against the precepts of Penguanitarianism, if, for example, a penguin says hateful things against other penguin species, is there room for him to be forgiven and readmitted to the group to take up once again the Love of Penguanity?*

Of course! Of course! exclaimed the Penguanitarians in The Council: for nobody was perfect, no penguin's plumes were ever immaculately clean no matter what they thought. Yes, where Penguanitarianism burned brightly like a beacon of hope, there would be love, there would be Nurture, and there would be forgiveness too.

Once again, the young penguin nodded respectfully when the Penguanitarians in The Council were responding to his question. And once again, he wasn't through with his line of questioning. It was as though he were asking these questions to reassure himself that he had not erred in his troubling conclusion. It was as though he were tobogganing a little syllogism which it would be hoped the Penguanitarians in The Council could clear up, could clear up any doubt therefrom or the niggling little consistency that was currently plaguing his young mind.

And so, he asked his final question: *if Penguanitarianism were universal, if it could be taken up by any penguin, no matter what his or her species or subspecies, no matter if he or she be young or old, no matter if they had sinned against the tenets of Penguanitarianism Itself*, well then, taking all the aforementioned into account, could not then The Elders of Instinct be welcomed back into the colony once they had recanted their sins, once they had gone back on the horrible things they had said about the King penguins?

There was a sudden silence around the fire. All eyes were still on the young penguin. And the black beady eyes of the Old King seemed to stare at his so ferociously, he thought that his stare would burn right through his skull. More silence passed before one of the Penguanitarians in The Council fielded this final question, which he quickly declared was a very sensible question, a question from a wise beak on such a young body, and the Penguanitarian said that of course The Elders of Instinct would be welcomed back if they were to recant their hateful diatribes, and that they had been given the chance to recant them, in fact they had all been given exactly three opportunities to recant them but would not, preferring to throw up their lot with the colony forever, preferring to go out and live in the open like barbarians.

This Penguanitarian then concluded by saying that as tragic as it was that there were penguins living a brutish life out there in the world, penguins who knew not of Penguanitarianism and therefore could not open their hearts to it, what was more tragic still were those stubborn old fools who preferred to bring up hateful legends and talk of two-thousand this or two-thousand that hiding in a whale carcass. Yes indeed, there was nothing so tragic as the penguin who had been given ample opportunity to embrace the tenets of Penguanitarianism but decided from stubbornness, from selfish pride, from hate in his or her black heart, from having a dark soul, to forgo it and instead to go out to the katabatic winds or dive into the stormy seas beset with killers whales and to perish. In a nutshell, going against Penguanitarianism was no more than suicide. But yes, to conclude the conclusion itself, the Penguanitarian proclaimed, his flipper wiping something from his eyes, the wilful heathens were never cast out by those who believed in Penguanitarianism; rather it was they who cast themselves out by turning their backs on Penguanitarianism, turning their backs on its love and its Nurture.

Thereafter, more questions were asked by other penguins. More basic questions. More agreeable questions. And then the meeting, which all agreed had been a resounding success, was adjourned. And so, with hours of daylight still ahead of them, and in high spirits, all dispersed, some going to tend to fires, some going to dig through ice and haul out last night's nets, and others going straight to the task of working on a new project that involved erecting four new igloos, one of which, it was now agreed among the Penguanitarians and the Greenies, would now go to the Old King.

#

And a few days later the young penguin who had asked about Penguanitarianism and forgiveness for The Elders of Instinct had disappeared from the face of the ice. His parents said that something had got to him in their igloo when they were out helping with the food distribution in the Food Wareigloo. A trail of blood went from inside their igloo to outside for half a mile and then stopped. Word spread quickly. The penguins, on hearing of this or going to see the trail of blood, were all on a knife edge. The Council at an emergency meeting, to allay fears that a murderer resided amongst them, some of the attendees even beginning to stare boldly at the Old King himself, brought forward two penguins who had allegedly witnessed the attack on the young penguin.

These two penguins claimed, with much dubious hesitation and stammering, that it was a rogue leopard seal who had come into the colony and ventured into the igloo where the young penguin had been. And although they had tried to wrest the young penguin from the jaws of the beast, it was all to no avail, the leopard seal dragging him off and away from the colony. By the time they had raised the alarm and dipped two sticks in oil and lit them, for fire was feared by leopard seals and was a great way of fending off the beasts, neither the leopard seal nor the young penguin was anywhere to be found. There were slight differences in each account from each witness, but these deviations were not wide enough so as to cast suspicion on their collective testimony. It would be a cold case. And soon it would be so cold as to disappear from memory. The parents were given a week off from work in order to grieve the loss of their son. The emergency meeting ended. And all went back to normal.

A few days after that the two witnesses who had given the account of the leopard seal snatching the young penguin away disappeared from the colony too, also never to be seen again. And this time there was no blood trail. No, this time the disappearances were as clean as the driven snow. At an emergency meeting called over these two going missing, the Penguanitarians, and even the Old King too, speculated upon these so-called witnesses, questioning now the slightly diverging testimonies they had given back at the last emergency meeting. They agreed of course that it would be impossible to know exactly what had happened and nobody could honestly even try, but at the same time they informed the crowd that both witnesses had hesitated a lot that day when giving their witness accounts, and stammered too, how both of them had stammered an awful lot! And at the end of the day, who had last seen the young penguin alive, the smart young chap who had asked great questions and had disappeared in a trail of his own blood? Was it not the two witnesses who had last seen him alive? And taking all of these factors into account, along with their now going AWOL, well, that could only suggest one thing: and that was that a leopard seal had not come into the colony. To be sure, in the trail of blood, in that long trail of blood that had stretched for half a mile, there hadn't been found a single flipper print of a leopard seal, a flipper print of any type of seal for that matter. No, the truth was staring them all in the face now. And that truth was that the real murderers of the poor young penguin who had been so polite and nice when he was asking his question about Penguanitarianism and forgiveness were the so-called witnesses. And, knowing the jig was up, knowing that the net of justice was closing in on them, both had decided to hightail it out of the colony. And although Penguanitarianism of course would have given them a fair trial and forgiven them their trespasses had they recanted and taken to their breasts anew the Love of Penguanity, it was probably fair to say that they had gone the way of The Elders of Instinct, resolutely turning their backs on not just Penguanitarianism but on all of those now at this meeting, all of those who loved Progress and who believed that Progress was good, all of those who were civilized and progressive enough to know that tradition was, when all was said and done, inveterately evil.

      Most penguins there nodded their heads at the end of every sentence that was uttered. They did not know if what was being said was good or bad; but what mattered to them was that it sounded good – and if it sounded good and was being said by educated penguins from The Council and the Old King who was unlike them a penguin of the world, well, then it had to be good. Other penguins though were scratching their heads and thinking: *how the hell did we move proceedings from a murder mystery to tradition being evil? And done so in such a smooth manner too?*

CHAPTER 5: A WILD GOOSE CHASE

The Emperors took two days of planning and provisioning their best swimmers, who were due to leave Antarctica and swim their way over those many miles to the island whereon were, according to the Old King, the last remaining individuals of his tribe, the last King penguin specimens in the world. The undertakers of this mission gorged themselves on fish and squid the night before because the plan was that as soon as they would find the poor suffering King penguins they would regurgitate this food for them since it was claimed by the Old King himself that his tribe who were stuck there were extremely malnourished.

Wives went down to the shingle beach to touch beaks with the husbands who were to accept such a perilous journey. And mothers went down too, their eyes welling up with tears, to see their sons off who had just come of age and felt themselves invincible and important and in no way seemed able to comprehend the dangers that no doubt awaited them – in fact, in such boisterous spirits were these youngster that they were singing right before setting off, singing in unison and with much gusto an old Emperor song called *It's a long way to Peck-a-nair-ee*.

Since The Elders of Instinct were no more, the knowledge just was not there in The Council for islands off Antarctica. Indeed, since the Emperors rarely swam any great distance these days, the up-and-coming generation knew nothing at all about anything that went far beyond the great continent. It was the

Old King who gave them directions. And there was something quite vague about his directions that worried some of the Emperors.

Had they known the hardship and foolhardiness of their mission, very few would have taken to the waves that day. Very few would have said farewell to wives and mothers and thought no more about it. And all five-hundred of the biggest, the strongest and those with the most stamina, in a word, the top physical specimens that the colony had to offer, took to the sea and did not even look back once at loved ones as they momentarily disappeared over massive waves and churning foam, and then disappeared for good over the horizon.

#

The island in question, if it was the one the Old King had signified, turned out to be a small one. Very small indeed. A chunk of rock in the sea in all fairness with high cliffs on all sides.

The penguins swam around the island a dozen times, looking for some weak spot in its naturally-fortified walls. Around and around they swam. And some of their party, a hundred or so, after such a long journey to get to the island, and now after swimming around it a dozen times, suddenly died from sheer exhaustion. Those remaining penguins finally found a spot where one of the cliffs was more sloped. The danger, however, lay in the current there: for it was strong beyond words. But nevertheless, they swam towards it with all their might. And oh! Such carnage! Such needless, needless death!

Nigh on a hundred penguins ended up being dashed against the boulders, their brains spattered hither and thither, some corpses' intestines getting draped around the jagged rocks and anchoring the said corpses thereto, the swirling waters turning a pinkish red hue with the foam. For those who remained now, the reek of death, a strange bitter taste, was almost overwhelming. And yet, the warriors that they believed themselves to be, soldiers of Penguanitarianism, swam on past their floating dead comrades and hopped onto those jagged rocks, and there clamoured up the cliff face until they were finally atop the island and could survey its contents, which turned out to be a big fat duck egg. Nothing. Nada. The island, now that they were on it, was in fact tiny, even tinier than it had seemed when they were swimming around and around it. They estimated that the slowest penguin could waddle across it in five minutes, if even that. It was just a polished slab of rock up there. And obviously there was not a single King penguin to be seen. And although the Old King had claimed to them that the island was plagued with leopard seals, there was not one of those beasts to be seen either. And so what to do?

Already two-hundred penguins down, tired, hungry, cold, some with light wounds, others with deep gashes in their flanks and chests, the leader of the mission had to think carefully what to do next. He looked up at the sky and saw the dark clouds gathering in the west. Those clouds did not bode well at all. If the sea had been choppy coming over this way, it was going to be a hell of a lot choppier on the way back. No, there was no time to waste now. There was no time for frustration from those beneath his command. There was no time to linger and end up with a mutiny on his flippers.

And so, when he told them to immediately return to the sea, to immediately undertake the return journey since time was now of the essence, the most diehard adherents of Penguanitarianism tried to convince him and the rest of them that perhaps they themselves had erred, perhaps the poor and suffering King penguins were on the island that they could see some twelve miles away. Sure, since they were already here, and since they had already made a considerable sacrifice in terms of lives and energy and time, what harm would it now do them to swim the twelve miles and check out that other island? But the leader quickly raised his voice to such suggestions and told those who mentioned that other island to stand down, to stand down immediately, since under his watch there would be no more suicide missions today.

As the penguins clamoured down the cliff, they heard not only the sound of the waves crashing against those grim jagged rocks but also the sound of blowholes. Orcas. Lots and lots of orcas. A school of them. If not two. They were circling a little way off lest they too be dashed against the rocks or beached beyond remedy. Yes, orcas were snacking on the penguin corpses that were bobbing in the water. They must have got the smell of blood from miles off. But here they were now, ever the sadists, playing with the corpses of the Emperors' former comrades. Playing with them. Throwing them high up into the air and then swallowing them whole. And it could be seen that the eyes of the orcas there in the swirling waters, waiting somewhat off the slanted cliff, were expectant eyes. It was as though the orcas knew the penguins' dilemma, knew that the penguins would have to dive into the water. And what orcas loved much more than dead penguins were live ones. Live ones that could be tortured for as long as it would take. Live ones that could give them entertainment until they died too from sheer exhaustion or blood loss.

Seeing so many orcas, the leader raised a flipper to the penguins that were following him down the cliff face and told them to drop back, to drop back and return to the top of the island. This time there was no dissent from anyone, not even from those ardent Penguanitarians who'd only minutes before almost started a mutiny over striking out to that other island twelve miles off. No, this time all fell back.

And up there atop the island once again, the leader surveyed all sides. The school of orcas, from what could be seen, were only on that side of the island where they themselves had made landfall. And it was decided that diving back into the water from that side was certain suicide for all who remained. And so, the leader said that they wold have to take a leap of faith. The others did not like the sound of that. But the leader told them that it was the only option. On the far side of the island would be best: for that was the direct route back to Antarctica at any rate. And furthermore, it would allow them more time before the orcas would have cottoned on to their escape. And so, it was agreed.

And as quickly as possible, though some had to be pushed off, such was their reservation about the feat, lines and lines of penguins waddled up to the cliff edge and jumped off, diving down into uncertainty below, the water as foamy if not a little less rocky down below. Of the many who survived this leap of faith, there were some who'd been unfortunate enough to land on a rock or hit off one under the water. But for all that, the great majority of them survived and swam for all their might back towards Antarctica.

It was about half an hour later when the penguins, whose speed and spirits were flagging, noticed a couple of miles back behind them the smoke that meant one thing: they would now most likely never see their wives and mothers and daughters again. The smoke was the water being sprayed through the orcas' blowholes and meant that the orcas were now on their tail, and being much, much faster swimmers then the penguins, would catch up and kill them in no time.

And that no time came in, well, no time. The whales were upon them, around them, beneath them, leaping over them and beside them, were all over the place. And still not a single penguin was touched. Was it a miracle? Or were the orcas toying with them as they toyed with all of their prey? To be sure, the answer was not long in coming. One penguin, who had been swimming as gallantly as he could, was suddenly swung into the air like a torpedo by an orca, and before he had the chance to fall back into the water, another orca shot up and swallowed him whole. Just like that. Easy-peasy.

Tobogganing down a smooth hillside sounded like a much more complicated task than this sport in which the orcas were now participating with the penguins, who continued swimming on, who continued diving down deep every so often in the hopes that that would put them off the orca's menu. Some penguins in their fear took to constantly diving out of the water, which seemed to be what the orcas wanted because each time a penguin did that he was immediately grasped in giant jaws and swallowed or flung, his body torn by the teeth in the motion, fifty metres into the air.

Of the hundreds of penguins who had tried to escape from the orcas' pursuit, only seven survived. Only seven. And they survived by playing dead. By just lying there on the surface. Of course some of the orcas nosed them up out of the surface, were probing at them to see if there were any signs of life, if the game could still be played, but being now stuffed from such gluttony, their stomachs bloated and expanding inside them, they finally got bored and swam off, leaving behind them a patch of sea that for a whole two-mile radius was red. Pure red.

The penguins who survived, now exhausted, some of which were bleeding from injuries, continued their way to Antarctica. One of the party went beneath the waves before the continent was even in sight and never came back up. Another gave up the ghost when they were a mere half a mile from the shingle beach whence they'd begun their mission.

And so, staggering onto that beach were five, just five, one percent of that which had set out originally. And still their misery was not over: for on the shingle beach was a meeting party. And this meeting party was not composed of penguins but rather of leopard seals. Indeed, leopard seals had taken up almost every square inch of that beach for breeding. Had they fiery sticks with which to wield against them, the Emperors would have dispersed the beasts, gone through them all like a hot knife through butter and got through such a scene unscathed. But they did not have fiery sticks. And they had nothing much in the way of energy reserves either. And so, waddling their way slowly through such a maze of crushing blubber and gnashing teeth, only two penguins ended up making it beyond the beach. And of those two, there was only one who would make it thence to the colony, only one. And his name was Plucky. As good a name as any, you may think. Yes, Plucky by name. Plucky by nature.

CHAPTER 6: TRUTHER BE CAGED!

This sole survivor made it to the colony at night. As was the protocol, he waddled his way – although at this stage he was more crawling than waddling – to an igloo in which resided two members of The Council. There, and out of breath, Plucky lay bare the whole sorry business, the failed mission, the failed mission that had really been in his view a wild goose chase from start to finish.

      The Council members were much perplexed on hearing this. Such loss. Such serious loss to the colony. The strongest and best penguins of the colony now no more. And what of the grieving spouses and parents and grandparents and chicks?! No, it was late. Much too late to be darkening the doors of all those igloos and rousing them from sleep with tragic news. No. It would be best to tell them all in the morning. First thing in the morning. A few more hours in the difference would not matter. And at least they could sleep now in the dreamy calm before the nightmarish storm. Yes, in a few hours the other members of The Council would be woken up and informed of the catastrophe and told which igloos to call on to deliver the tragic news to the bereaved. That way the grief and hysteria would not be collectivized in one single place at one single time. No, the penguane touch was best for this sensitive and possibly colony-destroying news. Furthermore, although the members of The Council would not admit it openly, they believed they now really had their work cut out for them to stave off a possible revolt stemming from this tragedy, this mammoth carnage. They implored Plucky to rest, and when he was gone, they began thinking up of the important speeches they would have to give later that day, perhaps the most important speeches they had ever given and would ever give. All in all, it was deemed a crushing blow to every Emperor penguin in the colony.

#

A few hours later, with an overcast sky promising little in the way of light for the coming day, The Council members fanned out across the colony working in pairs. As each igloo was visited, the collective crying and screams waxed louder and louder. It was indeed a difficult task to spend your whole morning relaying such tragic news to penguins you knew. But this the members did, and as penguanely and softly as they could too. All penguins were informed too, due to such a disaster befalling their colony, that the full week ahead would be a week of mourning. There would be little to no work done throughout that time. In the meantime, there was more than ample supplies in the Food Wareigloo to service all and then some.

#

That very night the Emperors held a private meeting, a private meeting before the public one wherein Plucky the survivor would disclose all facts of the failed mission. The members of The Council at this private meeting were at loggerheads over whether to hold the public meeting or not, and especially over whether to let Plucky relay details of the failed mission. The Greenie members believed the truth must be told, warts and all. Some Penguanitarians, however, were worried that Plucky's woeful account could rile up hatred against the Old King and also, and more important, rile up hatred against them, since they were the ones who had voted for the failed mission. In the end, and decided by a very narrow margin, the public meeting would go ahead.

And so, prior to that agreed meeting, those Penguanitarians who had not wanted Plucky bearing all to the colony swiftly flocked together in a delegation and waddled straight over to his abode, and there pleaded with him not to voice any anger towards the Old King later when he would be giving his account to the colony, since no doubt the Old King was suffering too in the knowledge that the remnants of his own colony were no more and all that remained of his subspecies were he and his six chicks. They besought him to do the penguane thing. To put himself in the Old King's webbed feet. And when they tried to drill him on what he was to say and what he was not to say, Plucky pretended to fall into line: for he knew in his heart that they would somehow sabotage or get the meeting postponed if they knew what he was actually going to say.

The public meeting, as it turned out, was more a closed session to a degree, as widows who had recently been informed that they were widows and mothers who had recently been informed that their sons had perished would be excluded from attending. *Best to let them all grieve in peace*, it was said.

Now Plucky was a common penguin. He knew nothing of diplomacy or tact. He was not accustomed to speaking at these sorts of meetings either. And since he was still furious at having witnessed such carnage on that now infamous mission, he was not going to hold back when it came to pointing the flipper at one individual. And, after having rested for many hours by the fire in his igloo, with patches of bare flesh showing, proving where he had had a few close shaves with the leopard seals on the shingle beach, Plucky took no time at all from the outset in proclaiming that the mission had been a complete farce. Silence fell. Then a collective sigh went up from the audience. Suddenly there was tension. A boiling tension that hitherto had only been simmering.

The Penguanitarians quickly intervened and asked Plucky what he meant exactly by the word *farce*. And Plucky responded with great sarcasm, asking them how since they were members of The Council, whom all considered to be learned penguins, how was it that they didn't understand such a simple word as *farce*. This caused much derision to break out amongst the audience and the Greenies in The Council, and the laughter only died down when one of the Penguanitarians shouted at them to put a sock in it and show some damn respect for The Council and its sacred traditions. Ironically enough, the one who said this was the same one who had pecked the eye out of one of The Elders of Instinct not so long ago.

Plucky, after having mocked the Penguanitarians thus, admitted that if he wasn't loath to give out a definition on the word farce, he would, however, disclose a synonym thereof, and he shouted it out: *Old King!* Yes, he squawked, the Old King was the responsible party behind this calamity, this seismic tragedy. Not that far-flung island with its fortress-like cliffs. Not the strong current and the jagged rocks. Not the orcas. Not the leopard seals. But the Old King: for it was he, Plucky announced, who had blood on his flippers. Yes indeed, it was the Old King who had the blood on his flippers of four-hundred and ninety-nine penguins, penguins who had been in the prime of their lives until being sent off on a wild goose chase to an island that could never have offered sanctuary to King penguins never mind leopard seals. And Plucky ended his tirade by claiming that it was only by a miracle, the freakish luck of Nature, that he himself had lived to tell the tale.

The Old King, who had been standing at the back of the meeting behind a few lines of bodies and was hidden, stepped forward He waddled his way to the very front and stopped. His small stature compared to that of the average Emperor penguin made him look very much like a chick in their midst. And since he was not physically intimidating in the least, many pitied him, and from their pity came always a sort of compassion, a compassion that overlooked all else. The Old King kept his head bowed low. Everyone there waited to see what he would say. Surely he would not be able to talk his way out of this. Surely he would now be expelled from the colony if not executed outright for having caused, directly or indirectly, a large percentage of death for the Emperors. And to be sure, some of them there were hoping that he would be culled, even though culling was not common these days, not since Penguanitarianism had begun to hold sway in all facets of Emperor life.

Seconds passed. A few of the Penguanitarians moved so that they were in a good position to stop any violence should such violence break out. Plucky, nonplussed by the Penguanitarians' positions, stared with much reproach at the Old King while holding up his flippers, as if to say: *C'mon. What do have to say for yourself? You who knowingly convinced us fools to go out there and die like plankton. What do you have to say for yourself before I myself toboggan you through? And if the Penguanitarians here try to stop me, try to hold me back from tobogganing you through, there'll have to be twenty of them. Nay, a thousand of them!*

But the Old King did what was wholly unexpected. He waddled over to within striking distance of his verbal assailant and then prostrated himself in front of him and wept. And never before had the Emperors heard such weeping. It was a sort of weeping that chilled the bone. And as he wept, covering both eyes with his flippers, the Old King pleaded for mercy, pleaded for mercy while also asking how such misery could befall an entire subspecies such as his; proclaimed through his shuddering body how now he and his chicks were indeed the last remnants, the very last remnants of the subspecies; how the leopard seals must have finished off the rest, probably the same leopard seals who were now lounging a few miles away over there on the shingle beach; but regardless of this dark day, the darkest day he had ever known, hearing that his bloodline was at an end and hearing of all of those brave Emperors who had perished by carrying out the all-important work of Penguanitarianism, he himself would not lay any blame on any other penguin, on any other species or subspecies thereof, since a truly penguane individual must, however difficult it be to do so, see the good in others, see the good behind all the barbarity; in fact, despite it being the Macaroni who had driven them from Tierra del Fuego, the Old King would love them even more, for one of the tenets, one of the ancient tenets of Penguanitarianism, of which the Kings had been custodians and which would now be passed onto the Emperors since they had proved themselves worthy protectors of that ancient yet progressive creed, but one of the tenets of Penguanitarianism was to love, to love unashamedly, more so your enemy than your friend: for love of a friend was a given while love for an enemy was a challenge. And, seemingly as a way to coax the Greenies present into his emotional speech, the Old King stated that The Greenmaker up there loved to challenge all. His true reward for all penguins was bestowed on those few who could love unconditionally their most sworn enemies and through that penguane love, through that emotional sacrifice, to convert them to love. And as the Old King said all this, he wept. It did seem strange to see someone weeping and being able to say so much at the same time. But the Old King was up to the task. He spoke in repetition. And he spoke in hypnotic cadences throughout those repetitions. He wept and wept and wept and continued saying things about his whole subspecies having been wiped off the face of the ice and how only he and his chicks were all that were now left and after them there'd never be another King penguin again and how as bad as that was, and it was terrible, what was worse was that so many good and penguane Emperor penguins had gone out to rescue them but all to no avail, a great sacrifice made by the Emperors, the most penguane penguins to have ever waddled over snowdrifts and who had sacrificed their lives for King penguins they had never known and whom they now never would know since both had been killed by the barbarous elements. And the more the Old King wept and wailed and repeated the same talking points, the more the penguins at that meeting softened in their thoughts towards him – many in fact became more compassionate towards him than towards the idea of their neighbours and compatriots and loved ones having lost their lives in such a needless errand. Because, at the end of the day, using logic and the solace that logic can offer one, they came to a similar sort of conclusion: although they had lost many from their colony, there were after all other colonies of Emperor penguins on Antarctica; but the Old King, on the other flipper, who was wailing and weeping and prostrating himself there on the ice, had lost his entire subspecies. As he had said, once he and his chicks died, as they would die since all living things must die, since The Greenmaker giveth and taketh life, there would be no more thereafter on this blanket of whiteness. No more King penguins in either Antarctica or Tierra del Fuego or any of the many, many islands in the region.

Plucky, however, was not taken in by any of this weeping or wailing or prostrating. All he could think about was the cold water. All he could think about was the swimming around and around that Greenmaker-forsaken island. The intestines wrapped around jagged rocks. The suicidal leap from the cliff. The orcas hounding them and torturing them for hours and then devouring them. The leopard seals on the shingle beach a wall of blubber and gnashing teeth. No, Plucky was smarting way too much to take in anything the Old King said or didn't say. And he went for him. There and then he went for him. He went straight for the Old King. And the Penguanitarians quickly jumped in his way. And all hell broke loose. Plucky pecked the Penguanitarians and the Penguanitarian pecked Plucky, and they pecked him where his skin was bare. And there was a blur of flippers. And then the Old King stood up to his full short height and screamed at the top of his lungs. And everyone stopped fighting. And the sudden silence was deafening.

And what had the Old King screamed? He had screamed at the Penguanitarians to stop fighting the survivor because he wanted the survivor to kill him. Yes, he wanted Plucky to kill him because he didn't want to go on in such a cruel world, a world that could wipe out his subspecies just like that. Snuff out all he had known just like that. And his chicks, he wanted the survivor to kill his chicks as well. He wanted the survivor to kill both him and his chicks since there was no point in them living since the tribe, the subspecies that was the King penguin, was finished. No point in prolonging the inevitable. Better to get it over with now.

And Plucky not in the least taken back by the request resolutely waddled towards the Old King and claimed that he would fain oblige his request, And throwing back his head so as to get one great peck on the Old King's face, a death-peck if you will, the Penguanitarians suddenly seized Plucky. And it did not take a thousand of them to drag him off kicking and screaming from the meeting: six Penguanitarians was all it took. And everyone stood and listened to Plucky's shouting and screaming until it had become distant and then no more.

    The Old King, standing alone now at the front of the meeting, waddled from face to embarrassed face, and pleaded with each one to kill him, to finish him off, to smite him from the landscape for once and for all since The Greenmaker Himself had already so chosen it to be; that the King penguin was surplus to His requirements. But none of the penguins the Old King approached and with whom he so desperately pled would oblige. In fact, all offered him a flipper of condolence and said that they were sorry for his troubles. And if there was anything, anything at all, they themselves could do to help him in his grief, he had only to ask them and it would be done. The Old King, on hearing this from all of them, clasped his right flipper to his chest and said that he had never been so humbled in all of his many years of life. No, never before had he seen such an amount of penguane individuals like these Emperor penguins who stood before him now. And he promised them that he would never forget their kindness. Never! Not till the day he died. And now, somehow he would trudge onwards because they had given him hope. They through their kindness and condolences had given him hope to strive forth. Somehow, although his subspecies was virtually extinct, he would muddle on and with their help, with all of their help, bring up each of his chicks to be as good a citizen as was each of these Emperors who were here now offering him their help. No, he would never, ever, forget them. One and all.

    And as he waddled off, his head still bent low, he made a pledge: he would repay them by putting his shoulder to the wheel, by ensuring that their colony progressed and progressed and progressed, and from which Penguanitarianism, like the warm beacon of hope that it was to all penguins of the world, would shine from horizon to horizon. And not a single Emperor when he had left the meeting noticed or cared to notice that after such a prolonged time wailing over his misfortune and that of the Emperor colony itself that the Old King's eyes were as dry as a bone. And not a single Emperor penguin noticed either that those same eyes were not a single bit bloodshot from all that crying. No, none of the penguins present could think of anything else but that of their sympathy for the little old fellow who waddled off towards his igloo and was in their minds…the last of his kind.

CHAPTER 7: TO HATCH A MURDER

What do with Plucky? The Penguanitarians in The Council were now at a loss as to what they would do with him. Surely, after his outburst and his attempted murder of the Old King at the previous night's meeting, there would be little they could do to protect the latter's life if Plucky were not kept in captivity. At the same time, for how long could they really keep him in captivity before relatives and friends of his would start petitioning for his release and at the same time would start asking troubling questions of The Council members themselves? They expected a mob of his supporters to rout the cage and guardigloo at any minute. Furthermore, the Greenies in The Council, in many ways ardent supporters of Plucky, were currently mulling over when to release him out of captivity. So time was ticking. Time was ticking. And The Council members really had become implicated in a very sticky situation.

Plucky's popularity in the colony was huge and he had in a way risen to hero status since it was he and he alone who had made it back to them alive after such a cursed mission. At the same time, the Old King was much regarded in the colony, particularly amongst the females, who wished to mother both him and his chicks in any way they could, and who were constantly making offerings of regurgitated food to all of them.

Attempted murder, if proved by more than four witnesses, had been a capital crime back in the day. Now it meant a lengthy time in captivity. No, there would be no public culling for Plucky. The Greenies would not vote for that, and, besides to do so would bring down The Council itself and mean that many of its members' heads would roll, and not figuratively speaking either.

Could the Penguanitarians execute him, off the record, then? Assassinate him? That too could prove risky as it had always been difficult to keep a secret for long in the colony, especially if the act had been carried out therewithin. But as the Penguanitarians, gathered in the abode of one of their colleagues, holding this session in the utmost secrecy, they bethought themselves all manner of solutions to their dilemma. But the easiest solution seemed to always come back to that of executing Plucky. It mattered not if the penguin in question had proved himself time and time again a model citizen. It mattered not whether executing him was the wrong course of action. All that mattered was stability. Stability for the colony. And although none of the members said it openly, they knew that stability for the colony meant their positions in power would continue unchallenged.

And so it was agreed. Two days hence they would have everything prepared. Two penguins, it was agreed, would carry out such a task together – cull and transportation of the carcass to the sea, where it would be left to the destiny of the carnivorous birds and the currents. The Penguanitarians agreed that it was a dirty business, this secret culling, but that it was after all best for the colony. And even the Elders of Instinct, for all of their palaver and superstition, used to maintain that no one penguin could ever be more important than the colony itself.

Yes, they would select two penguins to get the job done. Two was always best: for one would keep on the case of the other and stop him from going public; one would keep tabs on the other because if the other spilled his guts both would pay a hefty price for their action. The Penguanitarians went through a number of names. The names were of those whom the members were sure had no affiliations whatsoever to Plucky or to any of his friends or relatives. To be sure, they would have to be two penguins who desired themselves to be given something sweet and rewarding, perhaps to be anointed as junior members to The Council. They would therefore be ambitious and psychopathic penguins who would jump at such a chance and would be willing to get their flippers dirty in order to obtain their prize.

When they arrived at the two names that stood out from the rest, all members brayed, nodded their heads and shook flippers. It was done. There would be little need to talk further on the matter of recruitment. They had their penguins. Now it was only a matter of offering the necessary sweeteners to get them to carry out the task. And as they left the igloo, and before saying farewell to each other, they whispered and laughed about ghosts. It was a private joke amongst some of the Penguanitarians. Ghosts, they said, were great whistle-blowers.

And although the Penguanitarians did not say it as they went their separate ways, some of them were already contemplating how best to bring about Plucky's legacy. The great thing, they thought, about a penguin who was no longer in a colony was how his legacy, if they so wished to leave him one, could be moulded. His character could be sanctified or vilified, all depending on the whims of those who held the reins of power and the utility thereof. A great national hero today, they had often said while backslapping each other in joviality, could if deemed necessary become a traitor to that same nation over the following morning's breakfast table.

In the case of Plucky, they would do their damnedest to leave him with a bad legacy. Once they would receive news of his assassination, they would immediately inform the public of Plucky's "Great Desertion". And desertion was much frowned upon in Emperor colonies. For the average penguin in a colony, hearing of another deserting them felt like being spat at, right in the eye. Oh yes, the Penguanitarian members of The Council would pin desertion on Pluck and a whole lot more too. Indeed, what mattered above all else was colony stability, colony stability and their increasing power over that colony.

CHAPTER 8: ANOTHER PLUCKY ESCAPE

Now unbeknownst to the Penguanitarians, or perhaps a fact that they had foolishly overlooked, Plucky was in good standing with one of the captivity guards, himself a somewhat slow-witted penguin whose brother had been on the Mission of Death. And that same guard was due to be on duty the night of the culling.

The night came. When the guard, only a few hours into his shift, was informed by a delegation of Penguanitarians from The Council that he could leave in an hour's time since penguins would be coming to the guardigloo and cages to do some much-needed renovations, the guard, excited and naïve, went straight to Plucky to tell him the good news and that he'd see him on the following night.

Of course, Plucky knew what all this meant. And now completely alone in the building, the other cages in the corridor empty, he had to think of some way by which he could bust himself out of there. The walls of ice were extra thick and the corridor doorway was too tough to be charged down. The small panel at the front of his cage was lined with thick trunks of driftwood, there being only enough space to pass a single flipper through them but certainly nothing wider. His heart pounding now in his chest, his breathing thick and fast, he paced the cage, wondering how the hell he could make his escape before the death squad would show up.

And then he spotted it. He was surprised that he hadn't

spotted it before. On the wall to the left of the cage door and panel of driftwood trunks was a sort of ledge. A narrow ledge. Maybe too narrow for a penguin to perch on. But he realized that this ledge was his only chance. If he were able to get up onto it and somehow stay up on it, the assassin or assassins would not be able to see him in the cage when they'd arrive and peer through the trunks of driftwood. They would not be able to see him in here and most likely would open the cage and step in just to make sure he wouldn't be in here. And that would be his chance. His only chance. He could pounce on the would-be assassin and then flee. Waddle out of there as swiftly as his feet would carry him. And once out of there, he would not stop. He would not stop until he'd be outside of the whole colony. And even then he'd keep going. To the shingle beach. And thence to the sea. And thence to somewhere. Anywhere. Yes, the shingle beach most likely would be still full of leopard seals. And the sea would be beset with dangerous denizens of the deep. But he'd take his chances. With his last breath, he'd take his chances. And maybe if he survived, he could join another colony. A colony that was still in step with the ways of old. And he could tell them what was going on here. He could tell them of the dangers of Penguanitarianism and that treacherous King penguin. That maniacal old fart.

  The sound of keys jangling and a few sly whispers in the corridor brought Plucky to his senses. The flickering lights from two pieces of driftwood afire began to intensify, a sign that the contracted killers were getting closer to the cage. And so, Plucky tried desperately to scale the wall to that little ledge. On his first attempt, he fell back down and landed on his rear end. Desperately, he got back to his feet. On his second attempt, he met with the same fate. The whispers grew louder and the flickering lights ever more intense. But on the third attempt, Plucky just about managed to get onto it and, with all his might, to cling to the wall, which was uneven and therefore easier to cling to.

  The sly whispers spoke to each other out there in the

corridor: *Where is the jailbird? The jailbird isn't in his cage. Are you sure? Look yourself. You're right: he's not in there. Wherever could he be? Say, you don't think the guard let him go free. Nah! Well, we'd better go into the cell just the same. Just in case he's hiding in there somewhere. Nah, he's not in there. All the same though, better to be safe than sorry.*

And the door opened. Plucky could see the shadow from the firelight of the assassin, elongated and malevolent there across the marbled ice of his cage floor. He went to pounce but checked himself. And then the shadow moved farther and reached in to the far wall, the assassin himself and his fiery stick soon thereafter entering the cell. And just when the face of the penguin looked up to where Plucky was, Plucky pounced. He came swooping through the air and onto both penguin and fiery stick, his feathers becoming singed and that bare skin from the leopard seal episode burning from the impact. There was a hiss sound as the stick fell onto the ice, but the flame did not go out. Plucky was much stronger than the penguin and was able to knock him out with a few flaps of his flippers and several pecks. But no sooner had he put this penguin out of action than the other was on top of him, his one around Plucky's short neck and the other around his chest. Plucky could feel the air being squeezed out of his lungs and dived backwards, the penguin on his back thereby being crushed against one of the walls and going down, his head smacking off the floor as he did so.

The two assassins were now immobilized. Temporarily immobilized that was. And Plucky for a moment considered finishing them off. But in his haste, in his mind that was thinking and overthinking, awash with adrenaline, he decided to just flee. Flee as he had planned to flee: for there was no time to waste. And flee he did, waddling his way out of the cage and guardigloo and slap-bang into a blizzard that was as blinding as the dark itself. Feeling about and using his memory of the layout of the area coupled with his instinct, he made his way past several igloos. And it was some time later that he realized that he was fleeing in the wrong direction. Instead of heading towards the edge of the colony, he was going right into the centre of it, going straight towards his home, wherein lived his elderly parents. And since he was already within a stone's throw of his home, he decided to call in and grab some provisions and say farewell to his parents. Yes, this latter deed was essential now: for he might never see them again. And how could he leave without saying goodbye to the two most important penguins in his life. How could he!

  He entered the igloo and went in through the partition to his parents' quarters. Both were fast asleep. Both were snoring and stirring in their sleep. He did not have the heart to waken them…but waken them he did.

  His mother quickly provided him with a kilo of fish, which he gulped down. And his father gave him his very own spear, a spear that had been in the family for generations and which had been the most coveted tool back in the days of yore when the Emperors survived by hunting for fish and not merely fishing for fish with industrial nets as they did nowadays. Embracing both of them, promising that someday he would return and right the wrongs, would bring honour to all those souls who had perished needlessly and were now being dishonoured by The Council, and how he would also even up the score with that wretched little King penguin, Plucky left, his waddling silhouette disappearing into the blizzard that was now like a blanket.

#

Three Penguanitarians from The Council arrived soon afterwards outside the guardigloo, all expecting to see Plucky's carcass laid bare for them as had been planned, to see proof of the deed. And then before the killers would wrap it up in a hide and go on their long trip to deposit the carcass, the Penguanitarians would bestow some sort of honour on the killers so as to cement the deal. Well, that was the plan. That was the plan if all had gone like clockwork.

  However, on entering the corridor and seeing the cage door wide open and beyond its threshold two penguins who were sitting up and scratching their heads, the Penguanitarians were very disappointed. How the hell did he get the jump on them? How the hell did he overpower not one of them but two? What sort of idiots were they at all? A chick could have completed the task better than they. And now this Plucky fellow was out and about. And he could be anywhere. He could be a whole mile away from the colony by now. Or worse still, he could be at one of the igloos of a Greenie from The Council, telling them all sorts, all sorts that the Penguanitarians would have to deny vehemently. And worse still, he could be recruiting penguins at this very moment in time to come and slay them all. And what with the blizzard, it would be impossible to track him now.

It was decided that all they could do for now was to activate the alarm. Activate the alarm and inform the other members of The Council that they had a fugitive now on their flippers. That their prisoner had waddled out of the coop and could be anywhere. And so, the alarm was sounded.

And suddenly the door of every igloo was opening and sleepy heads were peering out to see what was going on. And the Penguanitarians with the assassins in tow went for their first igloo call to Plucky's parents' home. Surely they might know something. And if they did know something and were trying to be clever by not being open, other methods could be used to get them to squawk. Indeed, the Penguanitarians knew that if they themselves were capable of murder, then they were more than capable of putting the pressure on, of ruffling a few feathers.

#

Neither parent looked very sleepy when the delegation arrived at their door. Neither looked like they had awoken to sound of the alarm which had been mere minutes ago. In fact, the father was eating his breakfast when the delegation entered.

The news was broken to them, how their son had escaped from captivity, and the parents' faces were studied assiduously as soon as this piece of news had been disclosed to them, to see if they looked surprised or shocked. And although the mother did look surprised, a little too surprised for the delegations' liking, the father stared at them nonchalantly and said in a rather bland manner that if he saw his son he would let them know.

One of the Penguanitarians mentioned food rationing and how those who aided fugitives, even if next of kin, could lose their privileges to food and could end up in captivity themselves if it was found out that they were lying to The Council: for lying to a penguin was one thing, but lying to The Council was deemed treasonous. This seemed to startle the mother and she opened her beak but then seemed to check herself and said nothing. The father just kept staring at them nonchalantly and once again let them know that if he saw his son he would let them know. And so the visit to Plucky's parents' home had been more or less a waste of time.

#

It was, however, when the delegation was leaving the igloo of Plucky's parents, the blizzard now having stopped, that they came upon a neighbour the next igloo over. And this neighbour, an old female, was adamant that she had seen a silhouette leaving Plucky's parents' igloo and going off in a northern direction. Of course, she said, it wasn't easy to make out, what with the blizzard et al, but she definitely saw someone or something moving through the blizzard and going off that way.

Now, going off in a northern direction could only mean one thing: Plucky was heading to the shingle beach; Plucky was going to try to make it to the sea; and once in the sea, Plucky was going to strike out along the coast and to join another colony, a colony that perhaps was still living what was deemed by the Penguanitarians to be a barbaric life. The neighbour, who seemed to be delighted in disclosing this information and wanted to invite the whole delegation and assassins into her abode for breakfast, was quickly given short shrift.

The delegation spoke for a few minutes on what to do next. Should they just let the fugitive go and be glad to be rid of him? Because in fairness, as far as they were aware, no penguin lasted very long out there on his own anyway. And even if he did join one of the barbarous Emperor colonies in Eastern Antarctica, what then? And in most cases, no other colony would accept him. They would sense something different about him and peck him to pieces or expel him.

But what if Plucky came back? What if he came back this afternoon or tonight or tomorrow morning? What if he came back and slipped in under the radar and started throwing his beak about? And once this question had been arrived at, all heads in the delegation knew what had to be done. And since it was now urgent, not a second more could be wasted.

The assassins were told what they needed to do. Yes, they had screwed up, screwed up royally, but they could make amends by catching up with the fugitive and finishing him off out there. And besides, the Penguanitarians laughed, the plan had not really changed much after all, in fact it had turned out rather better when one looked at it objectively: instead of executing Plucky in the cage and then carrying him all the way to the sea to deposit his carcass, Plucky had inadvertently done them the favour of waddling there himself and therefore taken the need away for them to carry his dead carcass all those miles.

And now, if they did not dally they could easily catch up with him before he made it to the sea. And thereafter, they would be brought into the power structure. They would be brought into The Council by their good deed: for ridding the colony of Plucky was good for the colony – and what was good for the colony was good for all. And now, if the assassins could just go and get on with the task at flipper, the Penguanitarians had some dirty business of their own to attend to, that of burning down their own institution, namely, The Igloo of Penguanity.

And as the assassins left the delegation behind and waddled as swiftly as they could in the direction of that shingle beach, one of them asked about the leopard seals there, if they were still there, and would they be expected to traverse it if Plucky was in the water on the other side. The other assassin told him to shut his beak and save his energy because he would need it.

#

And the question of the assassin's had been a good one after all since they did not catch up with Plucky until they were some fifty yards from the start of the slope that gradually led down to that beach.

Plucky saw them and hurried up his descent by tobogganing, but the two assassins utilizing the same method of motion were gaining on him, gaining on him at lightning pace. And by the time Plucky got down to the bottom of the slope and was staring at a hundred metres of shingle whereon was a wall of sleeping blubber and teeth, the assassins were behind him and within striking distance.

He had hoped to be able to take his time crossing the beach, zigzagging this way and that, in a way dancing around all the potential threats from the beasts. But now he realized that he had to take his chances by waddling directly across it come what may. He realized that he had to take his chances with the sleeping seals more so than with the penguins. And so, he began the perilous crossing, waddling quickly but at the same time trying not to touch off any of the seals.

The assassins followed him, albeit somewhat more clumsily. And then it happened. Then a seal suddenly woke up and opened its jaws around one of the assassin's heads. The trapped assassin began squawking up a terrible racket altogether and this woke up more seals, one of which rounded its jaws around its feet, thereby causing both seals to tug at the hapless penguin until he was sundered in half and his blood spattered the cold shingle below.

On seeing this, the other assassin stopped in his tracks and then turned tail. No, no promotion to The Council was worth this. Nothing was worth this. And he was gone, clamouring back up the slope, squawking with terror as he went.

For his part, Plucky continued crossing the beach, his progress even slower than before due to more seals waking up. At the top of the slope the assassin stopped, turned around and looked. He wanted to see if Plucky would make it. He was half hoping he would make it and half hoping he wouldn't. The part of him that wanted Plucky to make it was, he considered, down to Plucky being of the same subspecies as he and currently up against overwhelming odds in a minefield of a dangerous other species. He waited some ten minutes to see if Plucky would emerge on the other side and dive into the water. He waited for what seemed like an age, not being able to see the penguin below in all that blubber and commotion. And then suddenly he saw something moving in the water. A silhouette. And there was no doubting that it was the silhouette of a penguin. Plucky had made it. His colleague had not though. And now as he turned back and started waddling the several miles to the colony, he started rehearsing in his head what exactly he would tell the Penguanitarians. What exactly he would tell them. And what exactly he wouldn't tell them.

CHAPTER 9: NEVER LOSE AN OPPORTUNITY

To go back a bit in time, a series of little events shout be noted, all of which starred the Old King. When the alarm was sounded, he was in his hut, but he was not sleeping. Instead, he was waddling from wall to wall in a sort of wee-hour ritual. And this ritual was one in which his kind, the King penguins, meditated, obtained solace, by moving back and forth with precious metals on their feet, tucked in beneath that flappy layer of skin. And the Old King had been performing this with his chunk of silver, some thirty pounds in weight.

On hearing the alarm, he quickly hid his silver in a little cubbyhole, opened his door so that it was slightly ajar and peered out. There were many, many penguins waddling hither and thither. And many of them were squawking. He could hear them saying that Plucky had escaped, that Plucky was somewhere in the colony. And he saw neighbours going from igloo to igloo, checking to see if all was alright. The Old King quickly closed his door and locked it. He went over to the centre of his room and thought about the situation. It was pandemonium out there. Sheer pandemonium. The Emperors were going about like headless chickens. And with pandemonium, if one kept a clear head about him he could turn the situation to his advantage. Yes, he would have to listen and watch. Listen and watch. For any opportunity that might arise.

And when the knocks came on his door, he stood stock still. No, he would not answer it. The knocks came again and still he did not go to his door. Voices from neighbours asked loudly through the keyhole if he was in there, if everything was alright, if he could just come to the door and open it so that they would know that he was alright in there. And still, the Old King didn't move. And then he heard the bodies waddling off and he went over to the door and peered through the keyhole and saw them going to the next igloo over. And then he heard them saying that they would go to The Council and inform them that the Old King hadn't answered his door and that they felt that something was wrong in there, very wrong. And with that, he saw all his neighbours leaving their homes and making their way to the centre of the colony where meetings were usually held. Perhaps this was a security measure for when prisoners had escaped their cages and were stalking about somewhere in the colony. And then they were gone. And then a few igloos down the Old King saw The Stonekeeper departing with much haste, leaving his door wide open behind him. And it dawned on the Old King then and there that there was a great chance of undermining the colony, well, at least the Greenie part of it.

And when the coast was clear, he swaddled his neck in a shawl of nesting, lit a stick from his hearth and, tucking his head down into his chest lest he be seen and identified, the Old King waddled down to The Stonekeeper's igloo and went inside.

And there, lit up by the flame from his stick, the Old King saw on a table that which he had hoped to see: The Sacred Greenstone. And without a moment's hesitation, he quickly seized it and pushed it in beneath that flabby layer of skin just above his feet. And before leaving, his eye roved over another object or artefact in that abode, and that was a whale tooth, sharpened by a penguin from long ago and thereby fashioned into a dagger. And the Old King pilfered that too without thinking twice.

Safely back in his own igloo with his loot, the Old King hid The Sacred Greenstone in the grate beneath the hearth. And then he picked up the dagger and took a deep breath. What he was going to do now was going to be painful as hell. But do it he must. Self-sacrifice for a greater good for the self. He lifted the dagger as far back as his flippers could reach, paused, and then thrust it deep, but not too deep, into his flank. A trickle of blood came out a few seconds after executing the act. And he waddled over to his door, unlocked it, opened it fully back, got down onto his belly and crawled across the snow and ice, screaming his lungs out, screaming for help, calling out to anyone who might be there to go and seek emergency services because he'd been attacked by a rogue penguin, yes, a rogue penguin had managed to sneak into his home and hold him hostage for nigh on an hour and had then stabbed him when he realized that the poor Old King had nothing of material value to give him, neither spare food nor freshwater nor anything else much of value. And his cries did not take long to bring several Emperors to his side, who carried him all the way to the centre of the colony, where at that moment of time the bodybird was with his family. And the bodybird quickly got the penguins to bring him to his own igloo, which was nearby. And there, the bodybird used all his savvy and experience to extract the dagger, which luck would have it was not in too deep and had not damaged any internal organs or any of the main arteries. In fact, when all was said and done, the bodybird said that the Old King had had a lucky escape since the wound was superficial and would heal in a matter of weeks once he rested and took in plenty of liquids and good food.

CHAPTER 10: A FAILED ASSASSIN'S PROMOTION

The failed assassin returned to the colony some hours later, exhausted and very much in need of freshwater and rest. He did not even bother going to the Penguanitarians to fill them in on what had transpired there on the shingle beach. His wife served him his supper and stoked up the fire. And when he lay down, she covered him in the warmest nesting that she had.

He was not long asleep when he was awoken by her voice. He opened his eyes and saw her standing over him. And she was saying that there were penguins here who wanted to see him, who were worried about him and wanted to have a little chat with him in private. And before he could tell her to get rid of the unwanted visitors and to let him get back to sleep, she was gone and in her stead were three familiar beaks over him. They were the Penguanitarians from The Council. The same penguins who had hired him to do that dirty job.

Well, cranky from fatigue and angry at failing his mission on two occasions, and not to mention seeing his colleague being torn asunder by leopard seals, the assassin would not waste time in letting them know that they could shove their membership to The Council or anything else where the snow didn't melt.

And when the Penguanitarians were sure that his wife was out of earshot, had gone outside to speak with a neighbour across the way, they asked him about his mission. Had Plucky been terminated after all? And where was his colleague? They'd heard it straight from his mother's beak that he'd not returned since the night before. And so, the assassin filled them in. Filled them in with both fact and fiction. His colleague had died, had been torn asunder by leopard seals on the shingle beach. And this piece of news didn't seem to upset the Penguanitarians in the least: in fact, they seemed to revel in it. He told them about Plucky taking his chances with the seals rather than taking them on because Plucky knew that he wouldn't stand a chance against both assassins without the element of surprise – to this, although they didn't really know whether to believe it or not, the Penguanitarians cheered and slapped the assassin about playfully.

      Yes, but what had happened to Plucky? Did the madpenguin escape after all? And the assassin told them that the madpenguin in question lasted all of twenty seconds on that beach before he too was torn to ribbons by the leopard seals. And whether they believed this version of accounts or not too, the Penguanitarians celebrated it nonetheless and told the assassin that for his hard work, for his resilience and his loyalty, they would reward him. In fact, they would declare him here and now as officially being a member of The Council. A senior member mind. Not a junior member as they had initially promised. Was he ready for his initiation ceremony? But the assassin knew. He knew what was coming. And he knew it was too late for him, given his current position, to do anything about it. And with that, the Penguanitarians seized upon his beak and kept it from opening. And at the same time they smothered his face with the nesting that his wife had earlier so lovingly covered his body with. And the assassin's voice being muffled, all he could do was struggle. But the weight of the three penguins on him was too much. And after quite a long time, because penguins could hold their breath for ages, he was suddenly still and lifeless. And with that, one of the Penguanitarians tore out of the igloo braying, calling for help, telling the wife that her husband had just had some sort of seizure and was now not moving and didn't seem to have a pulse.

CHAPTER 11: NO GREENSTONE UNTURNED & THE CHOSEN PENGUIN

An emergency meeting was called for that night. And all were due to be in attendance apart from the youngest chicks and their minders and Plucky's parents, who were informed by a delegation of Penguanitarians that it would probably be best if they kept a low profile for the next while until things in the colony had simmered down.

And that meeting, which took a long time to get started due to all the squawking and flapping of flippers and all the accusations, finally began in earnest. The Council gathered around the public fire and all twelve of them, now six Greenies and six Penguanitarians, faced off to the audience. There was much on the agenda this night. Much to get through. And some terrible news to be disclosed as well. And furthermore, what was important was that all remained calm, that nobody get dragged down into hearsay and innuendo, that all believe in what The Council had to tell them because the truth always came from The Council, and the truth always came from The Council because The Council always had the penguins' interests at heart, always had the colony's interests at heart above all other interests, whatever they might be.

First and foremost, The Council could confirm, not to anyone's shock that was, that Plucky had somehow managed to escape captivity and had fled the colony. No, he was definitely not still in the colony because every single igloo had been searched. He was gone. And when asked by some just how exactly Plucky had been able to escape captivity and if this meant that in future serious criminals, killers, would be able to escape captivity as well, The Council in unison allayed any such fears emanating from those questions, the previous night being a fluke, renovations there due to take place and Plucky somehow convincing the two penguins who showed up to let him escape, which they obliged, both leaving with him, and one feeling guilty for his crime and coming back to the colony to face the music, but so exhausted was this conspirator from his long journey that he had taken a fit in his bed and died.

It was then that some Greenies in the audience asked why Plucky had been put into captivity in the first place. Besides since the Old King that night had asked Plucky to kill him, could they not have classified it as attempted assisted suicide instead of attempted murder? And since attempted assisted suicide was still a crime in any Greenie's belief, the sentence derived from it would be that of community service rather than that of rotting away in a cage. And community service meant giving something back to the colony whilst rotting in a cage meant being a burden for the colony. And on the topic of the guardigloo, the cages were all vacant now and had been vacant for a long time since criminality had been extremely minor in the colony. And should not then The Council show a bit of Greenliness and close down that wretched guardigloo for good since only The Greenmaker could truly decide who was innocent and who was guilty. And on their deathbeds all penguins would only be answerable to Him anyway. And perhaps instead of knocking down the guardigloo, they could use it as a sort of community centre.

And this was where the Penguanitarian members of The Council interrupted that loquacious Greenie in the audience and expertly moved on to the next item in their agenda. And that next item was of a very, very grave matter indeed. It was about something that was, pun somewhat unintended, at the cornerstone of their faith, the faith even of the penguin who had just spoken about closing down the guardigloo. The Council announced, with much severity in their voices, that The Sacred Greenstone had been robbed from The Stonekeeper's, which just so happened to be, they reminded all just in case the fact had somehow escaped them, the same night that Plucky had broken out from his cage and fled.

 Now there was absolute horror and seething anger amongst many of the audience. They'd heard rumours of this, they had, but they hadn't thought them true. But now The Council was confirming their worst fears. And if The Council was willing to go on the record here and now and tell them this, then it had to be true. If it was official, it was true. And the Greenies started beating their own chests with their flippers. Up till now, many of them had secretly supported Plucky. Indeed, many of them would have secretly supported Plucky ending the Old King's life that night at that other meeting. And even those Greenies who did not support Plucky's attempted murder of the Old King had chosen to perch themselves on the proverbial fence and not to have chosen sides in the matter. But now all Greenies were sneezing salt, such was their contempt at the notion that one from their colony, a penguin just like them, had entered The Stonekeeper's home and waddled off with the most sacred relic of their faith. No more blasphemous act could have been orchestrated in their eyes. No greater insult wrought upon them. And many of them vowed to go out and search the ends of the ice and to not give up searching until they had slain the sinner and reacquired The Sacred Greenstone.

 And like a great stage play, all scenes being sequenced to the utmost perfection, the Penguanitarians in The Council shouted over the angry Greenies and the pretentiously-angry Penguanitarians in the audience to reveal yet more bad news. And the Greenies sneezed out even more salt. For what in The

Greenmaker's name could be worse news than that of His Own Sacred Greenstone being pilfered?!

The news was about The Igloo of Penguanity. Believe it or not, someone, and most likely the fugitive himself, had poured oil both inside and outside of the building. And that barbarian had lit that oil. And flames had engulfed The Igloo of Penguanity. And in no time, the whole place had melted. And all that was standing soon afterwards was a large puddle of water where once had stood that majestic and vital building. And the water had quickly frozen and merged with the rest of the ice. And it had looked like The Igloo of Penguanity had never been.

Well, on hearing this, though they had already seen it with their own eyes, the Penguanitarians in the audience went berserk. They started braying up to the sky and tearing feathers out from their own flesh. The Greenies looked on in disbelief at their counterparts now expressing their outrage. And on and on the Penguanitarians brayed. How could he! How could he attack that majestic building that was a beacon of hope not just for the Emperors but for all penguins the world over! Oh how could he!

But the Penguanitarians in The Council were quick to go on the record by saying that they would rebuild The Igloo of Penguanity. Oh yes. They would rebuild it so that it would be ten times the size that it had been. Yes, they would show all penguins that barbarians might be able to melt their places of worship, but they would never be able to melt their spirits of Nurture and hope. And so, as arduous task as it would prove to be, they would stand beak to beak and undertake the project. They would get it done. And they wouldn't stop there either. They would in time build even more Igloos of Penguanity within the colony itself. And indeed they wouldn't rest until there would be one in every single Emperor penguin colony. And beyond that until there would be one or a score of them in every single penguin colony in the world.

What had been anger and feather-plucking amongst the Penguanitarians in the audience now turned to singing in unison, rocking side to side as they did: *imagine no regressions –*

it's easy-peasy-yuh. Then let us all have a try. No more barbarians. Love and Nurture and Endless Fry...

Since most of the audience was finally in jovial mood, it was with much hesitation that The Council disclosed another piece of bad news, a piece of news that was foreshadowed by one of the Penguanitarians in The Council as bringing great shame on the entire Emperor penguin colony, great shame whether one would consider oneself more Greenie than Penguanitarian or vice versa, or a follower of both. Yes, this was probably the most shameful act carried out on that night, in what was now being donned *The Bleakest of Nights* in the annals of speech. Yes, someone had been attacked. Someone had been sleeping in his bed and he was attacked. And to make matters worse, that someone was a guest in their colony. A guest whom all admired a great deal.

And right on cue, in he came. With a crooked waddling stick and a gait that was even slower than hitherto, he began his approach. The Old King. His side plastered. The plaster bloodstained. And the audience fell quiet. He seemed to take an age to reach the front of the meeting by the fire where The Council was. But he finally got there, almost falling on several occasions in his path.

And the Penguanitarians got down and prostrated to the Old King and asked everyone else in attendance to do likewise, because an Emperor had tried to kill him on the previous night, and by prostrating now in front of the Old King, it would prove that not all Emperors were cold-blooded killers. Not all Emperors were thieves in the night willing to kill at the drop of a feather. And at first only the Penguanitarians in the audience got down and prostrated. The Greenies, for their part, were still in shock over The Sacred Greenstone and were not processing what was happening now. But when they noticed that The Stonekeeper himself and of their clerics had got down and prostrated, they all quickly followed suit. And once the Greenies in the audience had prostrated themselves, the Greenies in The Council, finding themselves to be the only ones left standing, thought it wise to follow the rest and they did exactly the same.

And the Old King decided not to wait for confirmation from The Council that he speak. Seeing that they were all down there and for once his small stature was above them, he immediately began to speak with all the colour and turns of phrase he could muster. And the first thing he revealed was the night in question, how he'd been sleeping, having a dream that The Greenmaker had chosen him, him and not any other, to seek out the Emperor penguins and help them along on their road to both Greenliness and Penguanitarianism, how although they had made great progress in each, they still needed a helping flipper from a King penguin, and how The Greenmaker had taken the soul of the Old King's wife as a way to ensure that the Old King's mind would be solely on his vocation, that of seeking out the Emperor penguins and teaching them all there was to know about both Greenliness and Penguanitarianism since the King penguins had been practicing that creed long before their cousins here had, and therefore to ensure that the Emperors would not lapse back into barbarism, He had given them fire, and as a sign of fire, a symbolism thereof: He had made an Emperor who was coming of age, who was transcending from the realm of chick to adult, be branded with the colour of that orange flame, and consequently on reaching adulthood He had given each the markings of His fire even more so and ever more upon their breasts; however, to mark out The Chosen Penguin from the rest, He had branded all King penguins with an even brighter tinge of orange upon the breast and oft too on the very beak: for the King penguin, The Chosen Penguin, was the saviour of the ice, he who served him would know The Greenmaker more intimately, and he who served The Chosen Penguin would find his place all the more guaranteed amongst the stars that would be caressed by his warm green curtain of light. And this dream was special. This dream had been created by Him. And this dream was created by Him as a unification of Greenliness and Penguanitarianism.

And the dream had been ending when the Old King felt

a painful blow upon his beak. The blow woke him up with a mighty start. And what did he see there lurching over him but the silhouette of a penguin, a large penguin at that. And in the darkness of his humble abode, the penguin told him to give him all his food and freshwater and nesting and whatever else he had of value. But the Old King had nothing to spare apart from his nesting shawl, which though offered was rejected by the burglar. And since he had nothing more he could offer, he told this intruder that instead of material things, he could give him spiritual satiation; he could tell him about the prophetic dream whence the intruder had woken him and wherein lay a special message for all penguins about salvation and progress and Nurture and listening to the teachings of the King penguin, namely, The Chosen Penguin, which thereby would his place amongst The Greenmaker be guaranteed. All he had to do was to leave behind this life of crime and barbarity and follow the teachings of The Greenmaker and His Greenliness and Penguanitarianism, a wondrous universal teaching of love and tolerance and belief in the greater good.

But no sooner had the Old King offered the intruder this than he felt something cold enter his body. *Right here*, said the Old King to the attendees here at the meeting, pointing a flipper at where the plaster was now. And blood had come out when the intruder had stabbed him. So much blood had come out.

How I survived to share with you thus must be a miracle. It must be because The Greenmaker wished it so, wished that I disclose the precious and warm dream of His to all of you now. But of course, only He will ever know why he chose me to survive. The same way he took away my very wife. And, again, in the dream, in that wondrous and wonderful dream, He told me that He had done that so as to further my vocation in sharing with you Emperors his message that will bring you and all penguins further on the road to Progress and thereby further away from the ice floes of barbarity. But yes, survived I have. And that dream I have shared. And the intruder, having planted a dagger mere inches from my beating heart, has failed. He failed and disappeared into the night. And though he is probably the same thief who made away with The Sacred Greenstone, though he tried to kill me, me, The Chosen Penguin, we must not slip into the whirlpool of hate and vengeance: instead, we must continue loving all penguins no matter what their crime, no matter what their upbringing, because it is only by love and Nurture that we can overcome the barbarity that is in this world. It is only by love and Nurture that we can reign in a new dawn of happiness and peace. And once that intruder is not in the late stages of Barbarian-reversion, there is still hope for even him to someday be redeemed. And now, my friends, my dear friends, I must waddle back to my abode and rest by the fire. I lost blood. Way too much blood. But it was a blood sacrifice. The prophetic dream given me by The Greenmaker had to be made sacred by blood, my blood, The Chosen Blood.

And as the Old King waddled away from the meeting, all rose to their feet from their prostrate positions and clapped their flippers in rapturous applause, many cheering his words, many cheering his message of hope, and many cheering simply because, unlike them, he was, after all, The Chosen Penguin.

CHAPTER 12: ACCOMPLICES OUT IN THE COLD

Life went on much as normal in the colony over the next weeks. The Igloo of Penguanity had been started and several families' igloos had been demolished so as to make way for the massive footprint of that building.

For Plucky's parents, however, life was not going on as normal. Other penguins shunned them when they were out and about, and they were informed one morning on going for their weekly visit to the Food Wareigloo that their food rations had been halved. Halved. Just like that. Why had they been halved? Well, the penguin there at the Food Wareigloo hadn't the faintest idea but that's what he'd been informed by his superior. And when Plucky's parents tried to speak to the supervisor, they were told that he was busy and that they would have to come back the next week. It really was rather odd: for the other penguins leaving the Food Wareigloo seemed to be carrying the full rations for the week in their flippers. And then they realized what was happening. They were being marginalized. They were being cut off from the social weal.

#

And when the following week came around, the same penguin broke even worse news to them. There weren't even half rations for them now. In fact, they could no longer get any rations. And with that, Plucky's father waddled all the way to The Councils' igloo.

He found there four members, three of whom were Penguanitarians and one of whom was a Greenie. He let them know what was going on down there in the Food Wareigloo and what had happened the week before as well. And instead of receiving assistance, he was firmly told by all four members of The Council that there would be no more free food for him or his wife unless they showed some solidarity for once and got out and worked for their grub like everyone else.

But old penguins didn't work, and Plucky's parents were both old. To be sure, old penguins had spent their whole lives working, and working very hard at that, so that they could retire in old age and draw in some of the benefits from that hard work. Well, that's what Plucky's father told the members. But the members told him that it was a new policy. No, there would be no more freeloaders in the colony regardless of age or physical incapacity. Everyone would chip in henceforth.

And so, Plucky's father, his body very much decrepit and arthritic, re-entered the work force, once again doing the most difficult job of all, digging ice so as to set and haul out nets. And Plucky's mother did likewise, taking back on her role as a preener, making sure other penguins' plumes were in good working order for the cold and bereft of lice.   And on one day, two months into his job, Plucky's father had a heart attack. He was half way down through the ice to retrieve a fishing net when he just keeled over. His workmates, who spoke little with him, pulled his carcass up out of the way and flung it into a hole in the ice some distance off that was being used by seals. And there it sank and was never seen again.

Not five days later, Plucky's mother, destroyed by grief, not knowing anything about her husband or where he'd got to, went to bed one night, and slept for the first night in a long, long, time…and never woke up again.

CHAPTER 13: GOLD IN THEM THERE HILLS

The Old King, having recovered from his own self-inflicted wound, did not have to take up any manual labour like most of the rest of the penguins. Instead, he began to go on very long waddles outside of the colony, his little body leaning now against not a crooked waddling stick but a rudimentary old pickaxe, atop which would lay a sort of sieve, and grasped in the other flipper would be a fiery piece of driftwood. And he would go alone. And sometimes he would be gone for two whole days at a time. Of course there were penguins who complained about this, who said that if he was physically able to go on such sojourns, surely he would be able to help with the day-to-day tobogganing of the colony as well, and with the loss of over five-hundred male penguins of late it should be all flippers to the pump. And when this was put to The Council, the Greenie members would say that he was doing The Greenmaker's work and that He was working through the Old King and only He knew what he was going to achieve through the Old King: for The Greenmaker worketh in mysterious ways, but, notwithstanding this knowledge, all must believe in His plan. The Penguanitarians in The Council when asked about the Old King's lack of work for the colony responded in a similar vein but more in line with their universal doctrine, believing that the Old King was trying to make contact with other colonies so as to bring to them the fruits of Penguanitarianism.

But alas, the Old King was not hearing any voices from

the green phenomenon in the night sky; nor was he attempting to reach out to other colonies – at least not yet anyway. No, and although it was said that penguins had little in the department of sense of taste and smell, the Old King, you see, had picked up a scent recently and he knew that scent ever so well. In fact, all King penguins were endowed with the sharp sense of smell for that wondrous thing. And that thing was gold. The Old King had simply followed his beak and come across a stretch of hills. And the hills, when the snow was scraped away, were all aglitter with gold.

It was tedious work to be sure. There were not large nuggets to be had at first. But the Old King showed an incredible vigour when it came to chipping away at the rock and a great intuition when it came to finding the veins that tobogganed hither and thither in that rock. Slowly but surely, he began to amass his fortune. And since his chicks were getting bigger, sometimes they would leave off attending the nursery for a few days and accompany him to those hills.

#

It was the first time in his long life that the Old King had done manual labour. And how he loathed manual labour. But each time he felt like throwing it all up and going back to rest in his igloo by the hearth, a sparkle in the rocks would catch his eye and suddenly his spirits were heightened once more. He knew what he was doing.

Had the other penguins found out what the Old King was up to, many of them would have scoffed at it, laughed like crazy, for, as an old saying that had continued to be in use right up to this day stated: *gold does not fill a penguin's belly*. Other penguins, on hearing of the Old King's enterprise would have become quite angry and expressed that anger to The Council, speculating on how all those hours digging up specks of gold could have helped to bring in so many fish instead or have helped to rebuild The Igloo of Penguanity.

Well, for all that, no penguin *did* know. Apart from the Old King and his six chicks, nobody in the colony was any the

WARREN O'HARA

wiser.

CHAPTER 14: BARTER OUTBARTERED

Now, it is difficult to sell something in a society that hitherto has known only food, shelter and the occasional bit of recreation, such as competitions for swimming, tobogganing and waddling sprints etc. that bring the community close together at certain times of the year. Once food and shelter are guarantees, it takes a bit of real craftiness, a bit of razzle-dazzle to get them to lust after other wares. Some, naturally enough, follow the trends as quickly as they appear. Others, however, are very stubborn indeed.

      How to convince Emperor penguins to change their ways was overall a slow task. A slow task but not an impossible one. The Old King knew this well. It was not something he had learnt but rather something he just knew how to do. Engineering the thinking and habits of others came to him in a similar way as that of a chick knowing when and how it must break free from the egg, or in a similar way as to how all penguins never tried to take to the air because they just knew that they, unlike other birds, could not fly. It was pure and raw instinct that lured the Old King out to the hills. And it was pure and raw instinct that led to him to commence doing manual labour for the first time in his old life. And it was pure and raw instinct that ensured that he would know how to convince the Emperor penguins that gold, which heretofore had no value to them whatsoever, would soon have more value than an igloo, more value than nesting, more value than fish, squid and krill, combined, and would have more value than even the air they inhaled into their lungs.

#

The Penguanitarians were easily convinced of the merits of gold once the Old King had informed them that gold would be a common bond between all penguin colonies of the world. In fact, in Tierra del Fuego, before the cull of his species, his brethren and other penguins too had been trading in gold for millennia. And, he said, gold was a valuable commodity because it was rare. Rarity, he claimed, made demand skyrocket. And the rarer that commodity, the more penguins wanted it and the more they were willing to give up so as to acquire it. And this whole process was what had brought such prosperity to Tierra del Fuego for so long. With prosperity came harmony. Gold was the glue, he said, that held Penguanitarianism and its penguane tenets together. Nobody could swindle another like they regularly did in the barter system. No, with gold, prices would be fixed. And nobody could try to squeeze out more from an unsuspecting trader or customer than what was the price, a price that was and only could be in weight of gold.

And with no longer the friction and conflicts that break out from parties feeling swindled, good intentions and love and fraternity would blossom. Good intentions, of course, were vital for maintaining Penguanitarianism. And the physical manifestation of those good intentions lay in gold. And besides, what was nicer to look at in your flipper than a chunk of gold. And what was nicer to the touch than the smooth cool surface of gold. And what smelt better than anything else in the world but gold – now, to this last statement the Penguanitarians were scratching their heads because as Emperor penguins they did not have the ability to smell much, and especially to smell gold as the King penguins could.

#

The Greenies were a different prospect altogether for the Old King, a different kettle of fish. If convincing the Penguanitarians of gold's merits had been a waddle in the park, then convincing the Greenies was going to be like extracting the spines from inside a penguin's beak. They did listen of course to what he had to say. The Greenies listened. They listened attentively at that. But the concept just wouldn't sink in. Why would a penguin, they thought, flipper over a whole kilo or ten of squid so as to be flippered back a piece of gold that was smaller than the smallest of eggs? No, it was a scam. Gold was a scam. It had to be. And they'd have no part in it. No part in it whatsoever.

But if the Old King was anything he was resilient. And he tried a different tact with the Greenies. And he declared to them that it was The Greenmaker's very Own voice that had commanded him to go yonder and seek out the gold from the hills. It was The Greenmaker who even appeared to him atop the biggest hill and called down unto him to complete the task, to bring the gold to the Emperors: for gold would enrich them since it was the very physical manifestation of He Himself. And therefore to disperse gold amongst the colony, and thereafter to many more, would be bringing that physical manifestation of Him to all penguins.

Gold, he declared with much passion, was not so dissimilar to fire in its colouring. And in a land blanched white, anything that sparkled or was colourful was a physical manifestation of Him and Him alone. Just like the bright orange head and upper chest plumage of the Emperors was a manifestation of Him. And just like the even brighter orange upper chest and head plumage of the Kings, The Chosen Penguins, was also even more so a manifestation of Him. And then, as he had gone into the topic of swindling and swindlers, so too did he enlighten the Greenies on that most shameful act and how gold, the physical manifestation of The Greenmaker, would quickly put a stop to that since He did not wish to see one penguin fleecing another and profiting thereby.

#

And therefore, the old barter system that had been in operation since the first ever Emperor had waddled across this great continent was about to come to an end. Gold would come into its own. And gold, all penguins were told, was immortal. Yes, it could be passed from father to son and from mother to daughter. And by such a manner could gold keep a family from going hungry. By transferring that material wealth from one generation to the next could all families be safeguarded going into the future.

The Council, now unanimous in their establishing gold as the system of trade and value, and themselves having received generous donations of the stuff from the Old King himself, went through the minimal motions by calling a public meeting. And despite a couple of voices of protest in the crowd, the motion was carried through.

Henceforth, barter would be phased out and gold would be phased in. There would be a transitional phase of forty days. And thereafter, it was declared, it would then be illegal to barter goods, all transactions being then orchestrated solely through gold. And a single voice there that kept protesting over said legislation was firmly rebuffed by The Council and told that if the Old King, The Chosen Penguin, whether he had been told by The Greenmaker or whether it was a matter of promoting the kind penguane morality of Penguanitarianism, well, if he believed that gold would enrich the colony, then there could be no doubting that it wouldn't. And if doubt there was none, then debate, any debate, there could not be.

CHAPTER 15: FASHION TRENDS

And gold at first was only used for purchasing food and nesting and homes. But the Old King, always on the lookout for new markets, realized that the Emperors, particularly the females amongst them, were becoming fond of gold. They were becoming fond of buying their squid at the Food Wareigloo or any such market, and counting out the gold they would flipper over. And making sure as they counted it out that the other penguins could see how many gold pieces they had in their possession. How many gold pieces one had showed how hard the male or female worked. And showing how hard or what long hours one worked derived therefrom a sort of social status. More gold simply meant more social status. And more social status meant that one was considered better in the colony than others.

What, thought the Old King, *if I were to sell them gold smelted down and shaped into ornaments which they could wear around their necks or flippers, or clip into the top plumes of their heads? And they would pay me twice or thrice or a gazillion times the price of what that gold was worth, simply because it would be a tad ornamental. Yes, the profits would be astronomical. And astronomical profits would mean getting back more of my gold: for it is all my gold at the end of the day.*

And so, the Old King set up a little jewellers' in the centre of the colony. The contractor that built the igloo for this jewellers' used a new design to mark it out from the surrounding igloos. And though the Old King went about the colony promoting this new little shop of his, the concept of penguins wearing gold just wouldn't take off.

And then the Old King realized that the Emperors were really quite dumb and backward. They could not grasp his idea as easily as he himself could. Either that or they really had no interest. Counting their gold pieces in front of others at the marketplace seemed like enough for them. Therefore, he would have to spoon-feed them his idea. He would convince them by making them jealous of each other: for what was better than something that was deemed by all to offer social status and could be seen on them at all times and not just in their flipper when buying food in the marketplace. And for the females in the colony, social status meant everything. They would trample their own chicks into the snow for even a smidgeon of social status, for even the suggestion of a compliment.

Now in the colony there were several really beautiful female penguins and they were admired by all and sundry for their attractive bodies and tidy plumage. The Old King approached the most beautiful female Penguanitarian and the most beautiful female Greenie. Once they agreed with what he had to offer them, he betook himself to their respective parents' igloos and laid out the offer from which the families would benefit – a whole month's supply of the best fish, squid and krill, which he pengunally would pay for and get delivered to their igloos. And for this gift to them, he would also bestow upon both females a beautifully ornamented gold necklace. For free. Theirs for the keeping. And all they had to do was hold on to these necklaces and wear them only at formal meetings, such as at a Greenie ceremony or a Penguanitarian conference. Wear the jewellery now and then and get a month's supply of the best food and the jewellery to keep thrown into the bargain as well. What female could turn down such a generous offer?! And what family either?!

Well, this masterstroke of marketing and advertising really did work a charm. In no time his little jewellers' shop was packed with female customers, both Penguanitarians and

Greenies, who had seen the girls coming into their places of worship and association and who had made their eyes almost pop out of their heads with jealousy. In fact, some of the females had become so jealous on seeing one of these models with the gold necklace that they snorted out salt crystals all over the floor and on whoever was unlucky enough to be sitting nearby. Gold necklaces quickly became the status symbol for females in the colony. And thence could the Old King introduce other adornments for other parts of the body, always advertising such new fashion trends with the greatest of pomp. And when young penguins were going to bond before the breeding season, it became an out-and-out prerequisite in courtship protocol that the male ask for her flipper in bonding and he did so by offering her a gold trinket from the Old King's jewellers'. And even the clerics from the Greenie Monument asked if the Old King could fashion for them a gold chalice since the wooden ones they were using looked too humble and drab. And the Old King, for the right price, obliged them one and all.

  The Old King was making a fortune from this trusty little trade of his. And he was getting back much of the gold that he had given when he had just convinced the colony that their future trading and prosperity could only be through gold. And for the common penguin, for the male in particular, these gold trinkets meant longer shifts building igloos or digging through metres of solid ice in order to set or haul out nets.

CHAPTER 16: NEW PECKING ORDER & THE PECKLES

Anyway, with gold came swiftly a multi-tiered hierarchy. Although hitherto, members of The Council, much respected for their verbal acuity and learnedness, had been afforded merely the privilege of not having to do manual labour, which the other penguins did, now they gained many more privileges. They with more gold in their possession were able to buy the best fish and squid and krill from the Food Wareigloo. And not only that, they themselves didn't have to go there to buy it, opting instead to use their PAs to go and buy it for them. And the PA was a completely new occupation in the colony. The PA was really a skivvy for the member – but even the skivvy for some reason or other had more gold at his or her disposal than did the rest of the penguins. And therefore, even the skivvy, although not being able to purchase the choicest pieces of food for himself or herself, was still able to purchase better and more nutritious pieces of food than could all the other common penguins.

      Life changed at a lightning pace under this new system of trade. Instead of penguins building each other igloos as they had done in the past, now a contractor came in with a team of builders. And he did not work for a yummy meal or work so as that favour would be returned to him if he needed an igloo built for himself or his offspring. No, now he worked for gold. And although he did less construction than his workers or no construction at all himself, he got most of the gold from the customer, the rest going to the builders. And if he was a contractor with more builders than the competition and had gained a reputation for being quick at erecting igloos, though igloos unsafe and liable to come crashing down, well then he got more gold and therefore was able to afford more benefits, especially benefits from The Council, than could the average penguin afford.

The Igloo of Penguanity was given much in the way of adornments, and gold was etched into its icy walls so as to show that it was a serious place of business, business and love at the same time. The Greenies, sensing that their creed was very much on the wane in the colony, paid with their own gold for a four-walled building of gargantuan size, bereft of a roof, so that they could gaze with wonder upon the stars and His green curtain of light and offer Him their praise.

And the Old King, who claimed to have dispersed all his gold reserves equally amongst the inhabitants of the colony, had in fact, and in secret, more gold than anyone else, more gold even than the rest of the colony combined. And having more than half of the wealth of the colony now amassed in his flippers, there was nothing the Old King couldn't do and couldn't get away with. He wasted no time in getting in the best contractor there was in the colony to erect a monument for the King Penguins, which he himself called the *peckles*. And unlike the other monuments in the Emperors' colony, nobody but nobody was allowed set foot inside the peckles unless he were genetically a King penguin, a Chosen Penguin. And so, it was only the Old King and his six chicks who could conduct and attend ceremonies in the peckles. To say it didn't raise a few eyeballs, this peckles and its blatant exclusionary practices, would be untrue.

Many Penguanitarians who believed in the universality of Penguanitarianism couldn't fathom how all penguins were welcome to attend their meetings in The Igloo of Penguanity but that only seven members in the colony were welcome to attend the ceremonies hosted in the peckles. The cognitive dissonance this arose in the Penguanitarians was grating, but ever the mental gymnasts they were able to explain away this contradiction by remembering that the Old King was after all The Chosen penguin, chosen in their minds not by some puff of green hocus-pocus in the sky but rather chosen by the abstract love of Nurture, which lay in a dormant or active state within every penguin in the world.

And on one occasion several Penguanitarians went to the peckles before a ceremony was going to be performed there. And they waited outside the doors for The Chosen Penguin to arrive. And arrive he did, much taken aback to see these Penguanitarians being so brazen as to stand right outside his sacred temple. But feigning compassion for them, he asked them what he could do for them. And they asked him why all were welcome into The Igloo of Penguanity, even into The Greenies' Monument, but how only he and his offspring were allowed in there beyond those doors.

And the Old King, speaking as though much offended by the question, broke down into sobs. How could they, he asked, come hither and ask such a question? How could they be so selfish? Did they not realize that he and his chicks were the last of his subspecies? Did they not think that since he and his offspring were the last of their kind that they had the right to have a monument of their own so as to meditate over the cull that had taken place in Tierra del Fuego and on that island whereon the leopard seals had lain siege to the last remnants thereof? Could they, as so-called penguane individuals begrudge him this humble monument wherein he and his offspring could gather alone to pay their respects to their subspecies before they, with their deaths, would mark the end of it all? How could they? Really, how could they come here and ask of him such a question? Their question went straight to the bone and caused him much pain and suffering.

And then, sobbing even more dramatically than before, the Old King told them that if they didn't mind, he had a ceremony to perform even though he didn't know how he was going to carry it out since he was now floored emotionally by their question. And he waddled in through the large doors. And the Penguanitarians, their heads low from such a tirade and guilt-trip betook themselves back to The Igloo of Penguanity, where they would inform the others not to question The Chosen Penguins having their own place since they were still going through the trauma of having lost most of their subspecies in the cull on Tierra del Fuego and the remnants of their subspecies on that island whereon the leopard seals had laid siege.

And the other Penguanitarians would henceforth give the Old King the benefit of the doubt in regard to the exclusionary practices of the peckles. And if any of them were gormless enough to bring up the matter again, the others would quickly remind that fool that due to all the suffering and trauma the Old King and his chicks had had to endure, exceptions could be made. Besides, without The Chosen Penguin they would not have gold. And without gold, they would not be able to stop swindlers from swindling and thereby undermining respect and empathy for one's fellow-penguin in the colony. And furthermore, as the Old King had told them, gold was the best way to bring the barbarian around to love since he was initially incapable of abstract reasoning and could only grasp the physical manifestation of love and tolerance and Nurture, which was gold. And having grasped that, gold would help them to transcend that hurdle between physicality and abstraction, thereby converting them from primitive birds into living citizens and exponents of Penguanitarianism. Nothing else in the world, he claimed, no other material, could melt a barbarian's heart as gold could, and once his heart was melted he would be susceptible to think in abstract terms just like them, the penguane penguins, the Penguanitarians.

CHAPTER 17: BEEF UP THE OLD SECURITY

Although the Old King was now incredibly rich and powerful in the colony and his position was relatively safe therein, he was overall a restless penguin. He was constantly worried that the Emperors would rise up, would get a silly notion into their pea brains that he was taking them for a ride or something. And instead of lying low and not trying to gain more wealth, the Old King tried all the more to enrich himself to the detriment of the average penguin. It was as though he could not make the connection between his getting richer and their getting poorer, and the connection between his getting richer and their getting more desperate, and the connection between his getting richer and their getting more resentful towards that wealth of his, and, well, the connection between that and rumours circulating by some of the plan to slaughter the Old King and his chicks.

What the Old King needed, apart from more gold that is, was security. And lots of it. And so, he got the most capable contractor in the colony yet again to build him the largest igloo in the region, and the igloo was to be built not inside the colony but a mile or so outside it. And once this monstrosity of an igloo had been built, the Old King hired six security penguins, armed with daggers and spears, to guard his property around the clock, three on dayshift and three on nightshift.

CHAPTER 18: A STATE OF IGLOOLESSNESS

Many penguins who had just come of age and wanted to settle down with their partners noticed to their utter dismay that unlike their parents and grandparents and great-grandparents before them, they could not now have an igloo of their own. The gold they had was only enough for affording them fish guts and the like at the Food Wareigloo and a rental space in an igloo with several other young penguins, penguins with whom in most cases they had been unacquainted. And every week at an agreed time, the icelord or icelady or a representative for the aforementioned would come around to collect the rent. Interestingly enough, for the cleverer folk of the working class, it was to be noticed that mostly members of The Council were icelords. In fact, it seemed that each member owned a score of igloos. And it was noticed too that he who owned most of these rentable igloos just so happened to be The Chosen Penguin. *Now how about that, eh?* the young penguins of the working class would say.

Other young penguins could never leave their parents' igloo and became depressed and were regularly squabbling with the rest of the family. Suicides amongst the youth, which had up until now been unheard of, began to skyrocket. The working class penguins who noticed the correlation between ownership of rentable igloos and the increasing wealth of The Council members and the Old King would often sum up this bleak state of affairs by affirming that all had been better in the colony when there had been neither gold nor a Chosen Penguin to introduce them to it in the first place. And these penguins, if they were foolhardy enough to utter such sentiments publicly, usually suffered some penalty or other for having the audacity and lack of Penguanity to make such spurious claims about the esteemed members of The Council and The Chosen Penguin himself: for without them, all would be living in a state of barbarity, without fire, without food, without freshwater, without nesting, still standing out in the blizzards with an egg half-frozen on their feet.

But these young penguins, once penalized a first time, learnt quickly not to open their beaks a second time, not to make such claims about the rank corruption unless it was in the presence of trusted kith and kin. Resentment in the colony, though very much in its infancy, had begun in earnest.

#

And as poverty grew within the colony, as some penguins even became iglooless, the Old King and The Council decided that something had to be done. Something just had to be done. A contingency plan had to be drawn up. But what could be done? Surely it was not their fault that penguins were becoming iglooless? Surely their becoming exceedingly wealthy had nothing whatsoever to do with their fellow-penguins becoming exceedingly impoverished? But alas! For all that, for all those talking points, something just had to be done.

And that was when the Old King, who had practiced the trade in Tierra del Fuego and the Falkland Islands and South Georgia Island and South Sandwich Islands and amongst many other far-flung places, and who had practiced it well at that, advised The Council to introduce it post-haste, to wit, usury.

CHAPTER 19: USURY

Usury? they asked.

Oh yes, usury. The solution to all financial problems. A good way, the only way, to bring back equality and tolerance and Nurture to the colony.

Those who were struggling to get their own igloos built, well, instead of trying to save up their few pieces of gold over a number of seasons, they could take out a loan which the Old King himself, in his kindness and penguaneness, would offer them, so long as the other penguin in each loan kept up his or her payments, which obviously came with high rates of interest.

The great thing about usury, The Old King explained in a closed session with members of The Council, was that the lender could not lose. If the penguin taking out the loan had any collateral at all, and/or had a relative or friend who could act as their guarantor for that loan should the original penguin screw up with the repayments, then the lender, namely the Old King or some member of The Council who might wish to get in on this soon-to-be flourishing trade on the ground floor, risked nothing, risked absolutely nothing. Because if the borrower came up short one week, couldn't pay the interest for example, then the lender had every right to simply take the igloo for himself and/or the property of the guarantor while he was at it. It wasn't just a win-win situation, said the Old King. It was a win-win-win situation.

It was as easy a business as swimming with the current, the Old King chuckled. Of course some of the Penguanitarians wondered if such a practice were ethically sound: for taking someone's home because they had fallen on hard times did not appear to be part and parcel of any of their lessons in Nurture and Penguanitarianism. But the Old King was able to waddle his way out of this as well. His black beady eyes twinkled as he explained how there was such a thing in Penguanitarianism, well at least on Tierra del Fuego when he'd lived there, which when all was said and done was the original home of Penguanitarianism, but there was such a thing as Barbarian-reversion. Barbarian reversion? they asked, recoiling as they uttered it, even though they had heard him using the expression before and were still unsure of what it meant.

Oh yes, the Old King went on to explain, *nothing so bad and depressing as Barbarian-reversion, the process by which a penguin begins to lust after poverty, lusts after anarchy and starvation, lusts after the end of civilization, and consciously or subconsciously, goes about trying to bring the system down by opening up the soft underbelly of a colony to a barbaric state of affairs. Yes, there is nothing as dangerous to Progress and Nurture and Penguanitarianism as a Barbarian-reverter. And if one takes out a loan for an igloo, it is expected by us that he or she do so in good faith. If however, they do not keep up their side of the bargain and do not pay what is expected of them, then it can only be presumed that Barbarian-reversion is begun within them. And once it is begun, it is very difficult to stop the rot. There is only one final solution to a penguin who has shirked their financial duties. Only one.*

And the members of The Council flocked around the Old King, their bodies bent over to listen to his voice that had now lowered to a whisper. Yes, there was only one final solution, and that was to offer them a loan so as to help towards paying the missed week in the original loan. But since this loan was an even more benevolent one from the lender, the interest on it had to be even higher. And all the members of The Council, all self-proclaimed Penguanitarians who preached about love and Penguanity and Nurture from dawn to dusk, and who happened to be icelords and iceladies too, slapped the Old King gently on the back and told him that usury was a great thing because *he* had told them it was a great thing, and unlike them he was a penguin of the world, well-travelled and knowledgeable as a result of that travelling. And once they as lenders of the loan could not lose their investment but had everything to gain, usury would become the best thing since sliced squid.

Now, there was one member in The Council there, a Greenie, the only Greenie left nowadays in The Council, who, unlike the rest, did not have a large property portfolio, instead having one single rentable igloo. Some said he was under the influence of a drug or other because he guffawed at what the Old King had just said about usury, and he did so by pointing out that if a penguin was trying to climb out of a hole in the ice, making that hole deeper was not going to help.

But the wily Old King was ready for this. It was as if he had had the exact same conversation with other penguins eons ago. Like he was going through the same old rehearsal, but one that never bored him. And his beady black eyes sparkled even more with a feverish joy when the analogy of the hole in the ice had been put to him. He explained to that penguin that Barbarian-reversion, or demonic possession if the Greenie preferred that term, had to be put to the test. Offering the second loan was the litmus test. If the penguin could not pay this second loan, could not reach out for the flipper that was trying to pull him or her out of the stormy sea, then it could be concluded that the penguin was a busted ticket, a no-hoper, and had given himself or herself up to Barbarian-reversion, or, if the Greenie preferred it to be stated in his own faith, that of The Anti-Greenmaker, he who dwelleth beneath all ice, once a favoured servant of Him serving on His left flipper side and who for betraying Him had been thrown from the sky and had fallen through the ice, and deep down there had been residing ever since, in eternal darkness.

And what then? the same penguin asked, unperturbed by talk of the Anti-Greenmaker. *What lies in store for the penguin who cannot repay that second loan, a loan which has even higher interest than the first one has?*

Well, the Old King said as he began waddling away from them and on to other pressing business, penguanal business, then all hope would be lost for that penguin. Then Barbarian-reversion or The Anti-Greenmaker had taken over and the original penguin, as all would have known him or her, was no more. And there could be no place in the colony for Barbarian-reverters or The Anti-Greenmaker. Yes, they would have to be expelled post-haste: for it was like a virus or an untended fire that could spread at any moment.

Of course, the Old King explained, stopping and looking back at the members of The Council as he did so, of course some penguins would think that inpenguane, the idea of expelling another for not keeping up payments. And he himself could understand how they would think like that – he too used to think like that in his younger days. But what the penguins, the penguane penguins, would be overlooking would be the fact that someone who had reverted to barbarianism, someone in the late stages thereof, could never be brought back to the tenets of Penguanitarianism. A barbarian could be converted, the Old King said. But a Barbarian-reverter could not. And if the colony became full of Barbarian-reverters, or, for the one Greenie present, various demonic manifestations of The Anti-Greenmaker, they, the civilized penguins remaining, all might as well throw themselves into the mercy of the sea, slap bang into a school of killer whales. And what would be more, they'd probably fare better with those whales.

#

The Greenies for their part, as they congregated in the Greenie Monument, did not like what they heard from the Greenie member of The Council when it came to usury. In fact, so despondent were they about it that they intended to use all their clout in defying any such trade to be implemented in the colony. Their belief system, though similar in many ways to that of the Penguanitarians' with its cornerstones of Nurture and Penguanity, had developed very much in constant preaching of poverty and how poverty was evil, how anything that increased poverty was spitting in The Greenmaker's curtain of green light. Yes, one of the clerics lectured, there was nothing that rankled Him more than seeing penguins without igloos, penguins going hungry and penguins taking their own lives because they could see no ray of light on the horizon. If winters were long in Antarctica, they were longer for the poor and the needy. And when one of the male congregants there asked the clerics, given what they had just lectured on, if they would not sell the Order's many gold chalices for food and for igloos for the iglooless, he was quickly shushed by the rest of the congregation, who had never heard such sacrilegious and insolent talk in all their lives.

#

He who pays the piper calls the tune. And the Old King was the biggest donor by far to the Greenie Monument. He put more gold into their coffers than did all of the Greenies themselves combined and multiplied by ten. And the Old King knew that the last bulwark against his taking over the colony lock, stock and barrel, was the Greenies. And when one of his informants from the congregation relayed the news to him that they would not accept in any way, shape or form, usury in the colony, the Old King swore an oath that he would destroy that Order, and he would destroy it once and for all.

#

Whereas his influence over the Penguanitarians was unwavering and without challenge, his influence over the Greenies was at an all-time low due to their rejection of gold-lending – that despite their order being laden with his gold. No, the Old King would need to take a different tact with the Greenies. And if he couldn't communicate with them from a material perspective, he would have to immerse himself once again in their silly superstitions. He would have to do something miraculous, something that would remind them that he was The Chosen Penguin after all; that he was their saviour sent to them by Him, The Greenmaker, so as to bring them the fruits of having believed in Him and having paid homage to Him alone.

The Council, notwithstanding that one Greenie member out of the twelve, was his toy army. And soon, the Old King would ensure the ousting of that one Greenie, who would be replaced with the Greenie who was really the Old King's messenger penguin, his informant. They would have to be convinced yet again that the Old King really was The Chosen Penguin and not some sort of Anti-Greenmaker, which of late the Greenies were starting to call him.

And so, the Old King betook himself one day to the shingle beach, and there high up on that beach and out of reach of high tide did he conceal beneath some pebbles something that, though having little in material value, had much in terms of sentimental and spiritual value for others.

CHAPTER 20: A MIRACLE WITH INTEREST

The following day the Old King went to the Greenie Monument and appeared much agitated. He asked one of the senior clerics if he would be so kind as to let him speak to the congregation: for he had had the night before a prophetic dream. Though hesitant to let the Old King speak, the senior cleric, fearing somewhat the power and influence of his agitated visitor, obliged him. And the Old King waddled up the steps, cleared his throat and began to speak with much urgency, but at the same time with much clarity:

In his dream, The Greenmaker had come down onto the ice in the middle of the colony. And He was angry. He was angry with both The Chosen Penguin and the Greenies. He was angry because there were so many penguins now without homes, without food and, most important, without hope. *And why*, The Greenmaker had asked The Chosen Penguin, *why hast thou forsaken them? Why hast thou not offered them loans? And why hast thou not offered them more loans to aid with the original loans?*

A few penguins in the congregation had to pinch themselves so as not to shout out in disgust at the Old King up there with his spiel on loans and loans on loans and loans on loans on loans. A few others there were about to stand up and waddle out of the Greenie Monument as a way of protest, to show their own disgust at the blasphemous thing that was being uttered.

The Old King though, picking up that the air around him was now very tense, nonetheless kept up his telling of the dream. And so, the Old King had explained to The Greenmaker that the Greenies would not accept loans in their community if those loans were capped with interest. *But why*, The Greenmaker had roared like thunder, *why will they not accept interest? Do not they know that time is golden? And not only is time golden but it is gold. For when the gold is not in one's flipper, opportunities are whizzing by like snowflakes and they are lost and lost forever. Why should a kind-hearted penguin who has loaned what he has out to another not receive some sort of benefit therefrom, even though it be a trifle when all is said and done, even though it be a quarter or a third or a half of the loan itself? How could one penguin begrudge another the right to earn from the loss of his golden time? Willst thou not speak with them, O Chosen Penguin? Willst thou not speak with them on my behalf? And willst thou not implore them to see sense and by usury to help their brothers and sisters gain shelters from the blizzards and food for their stomachs?*

Five penguins in the congregation stood up at once. They didn't leave. But they were ready to do so. They waited though to hear the next few words that would come out of the Old King's beak. And if those words happened to be about Him promoting usury even more to the Old King in that dream, which sounded altogether blasphemous, they would leave in quite a lively manner.

And the Old King, The Chosen Penguin, had promised The Greenmaker that he would do his utmost to carry forth His message about usury to them, even though a great many of them had closed their hearts to such sacred wisdom and advice, even though usury had been at the centre of all Greenmaker-fearing colonies since the beginning. And to show His benevolence to them, to offer them a sign, a token, The Greenmaker told The Chosen Penguin where they could find The Sacred Greenstone and how it had slipped by His will out of the flipper of a deserter, a brigand and a manifestation of The Anti-Greenmaker as well, and had there languished ever since.

Well if the entire congregation didn't half gasp when they heard this. *The Sacred Greenstone! Our Sacred Greenstone! Brought back unto us! Our praise be praised by Him! What is lost He recovers! What is robbed only He can restore.* And those five penguins that were standing quickly lay back down on their bellies.

And The Greenmaker had spoken more in that dream. And The Chosen Penguin had listened: *where water gush and turneth white, beneath some stones it sparkle bright.* And with that The Chosen Penguin had been carried up in the sky by His green curtain of light and thither to the shingle beach, whereupon He had pointed out to The Chosen Penguin its location or thereabouts. Yes, The Sacred Greenstone which had been lost would now be found.

And with that the Old King left the Greenie Monument. And the whole congregation followed him. And some Penguanitarians out of curiosity joined behind the line of Greenies. And slowly, ever so slowly, his waddling-stick in flipper, the Old King led them to the shingle beach. And along the journey the Greenies sang to their hearts' content. *Oh yes*, they all agreed, *if we find The Sacred Greenstone there, then it is a sure sign from Him that we must do His will and ring in usury across the colony, which He, and only He, had commanded to The Chosen Penguin. And if He said that usury would help to get our brethren out of igloolessness and hunger and into warmth and satiation, and if we find The Sacred Greenstone, then it will have been no dream of The Chosen Penguin's but a prophetic dream; however, if on the other flipper this turns out to be a wild goose chase, then woe betide the treacherous King penguin, the wizened old fogey. Woe betide him.* But of course, none of them really wanted to believe that this was a fool's errand. To be sure, all wanted to recover The Sacred Greenstone, especially the clerics and The Stonekeeper himself, the latter having lost much of his prestige within their circle with the absence stone. They knew with that back in their midst their Order would flourish; that those who had left the Order after that The Bleakest of Nights would come back and attend services, would once again stare up at His beautiful displays in the night sky and pay homage thereto.

All the penguins spread out across the shingle beach and began uplifting pebbles. The Old King for his part, not wanting to make it look too obvious, pretended to labour at the opposite side to which he knew The Sacred Greenstone to be. And while searching, he even took a bit of time out to check out a glacier that from a certain angle looked like in weeks or months from now would be breaking off from the land and forming a massive iceberg. And then he returned to the shingle beach and resumed pretending to search. But after an hour of pretending, he slowly waddled his way to where The Sacred Greenstone really was and uncovered it. He brayed out words of joy so loudly that all penguins immediately ceased their work. And holding The Sacred Greenstone aloft in his flipper, the Old King said as poignantly as he could muster: *The Greenmaker giveth. The Greenmaker giveth. Through me, The Chosen Penguin, dost he offer this token. Let us not linger here any longer. Let us return to the Greenie Monument. By the necessary ceremony there, I shall penguanally put The Sacred Greenstone in its rightful place there, which shall be in the flippers of The Stonekeeper.*

And The Stonekeeper, who had been searching more assiduously than any penguin on the shingle beach, and who was breathing heavily from his exertions, gushed on hearing this and began sobbing with joy. And with that, a great cheer rang out and a thunderous applause. The Greenmaker had bestowed upon them once again His bounty. He had given them gold which, though originally frowned upon, was now considered good. Likewise He had given them fire and it was good. He had given them The Chosen penguin and he was good. And now, through the deeds of one goodness had they been able to recover that other goodness, that other physical manifestation of His presence amongst them, whether it be night or day, whether the sky be cloudy or bright, The Sacred Greenstone.

#

A meeting was called the next day. All twelve members of The Council cast their votes. All penguins in the audience gave their approval. And it was a resounding success for some of them, and in particular for the Old King. The Penguanitarians said it was a good day for Penguanitarianism. And the Greenies said it was a good day for Greenies who had carried out the wants and desires of The Greenmaker.

Henceforth, usury would be practiced in the colony.

CHAPTER 21: GO WEST, MY SONS!

As many, many seasons passed, the Old King's three male chicks came of age, losing their downy feathers in the moulting process for those of adulthood, bright orange dashes around their throats, on the side of their heads and even on their beaks. Like their father, the male offspring did not like manual labour. They did not like being outdoors either.

They had helped their father to a great deal with the counting of his gold and the managerial tasks of sending henchpenguins to igloos to evict the residents who had not kept up their rent or loan payments. And they had helped with the managerial tasks too that had involved sending those same henchpenguins to beat up and occasionally murder a penguin who was a bit too flappy with his beak when it came to their father's business interests.

There were many rumours abounding about those male King penguins. One thing that could be noticed if one looked closely enough was that a little chunk of their cloacae was each amiss. Some put the rumour out there in the colony that strange practices were afoot behind the closed doors of the peckles and that the Old King had some time ago performed a ritual on all three of his sons whereby he had pecked off and eaten the cloaca flesh and drunk the blood that had spurted out from the wound. Of course many penguins laughed on hearing this rumour. And many more rolled their eyes and said that that was such a made-up story. Surely nobody in the world, whatever the ritual, would peck at their own sons' cloacae and devour the piece that they had pecked off and drink the blood from the wound. What good if any could such a monstrous ceremony serve? No, it had to be nonsense. Utter claptrap. The missing part of their cloacae could be put down to frostbite: for it was well known that King penguins were not as well adapted to the harsh climate of Antarctica as were the Emperors. Indeed, all Kings, including the Old King himself, had to swaddle themselves with nesting when outdoors, and even when waddling long distances.

But now the time had come for the King penguin males to leave the colony. At least for a while anyway. Nobody could understand this of course. Why would they leave? Why would they who despised being outdoors and away from their creature comforts set off on a journey? And depending on who asked the Old King this question, the answer was different on each occasion:

They were leaving the colony because The Greenmaker had told him in a dream to send the young lads out to preach His word and His love.

They were leaving the colony to convert those other barbarous colonies to the tenets of Penguanitarianism and how all penguins had within them the ability to become civilized and penguane just like the Emperors in this colony.

They were leaving the colony in a bid to search the world for any remaining King penguins there might be and, if successful, would try to breed with them to save their subspecies from what was looking like certain extinction.

Whichever were the reason, the Old King's sons did leave the colony on one sunny morning and would not be heard of again in quite a long time.

CHAPTER 22: INCEST OR WAKWAK RAPE OR THE SPOTLESS FERTILIZATION

More seasons passed. The rich got richer. And despite usury being deemed helpful and charitable by the powers-that-be, the poor just kept getting poorer. The Old King's youngest chicks, all three being females, moulted. They too were now of age, taking on the correct plumage of adulthood. And it was pondered by the other penguins, who found them to be in no way sexually attractive, if an Emperor could in fact even breed with a King, since both subspecies were not the same and yet were considered cousins.

Often this question was posed to the bodybird, who would respond by opining that such a union would be doomed to fail since if any egg could be fertilized and if any hatchling could hatch, the mutant penguin would have no end of maladies and afflictions and would most likely never be able to reach adulthood, and even reaching adulthood the probability of it being about as sterile as an icicle would be high, very high.

And many wondered what a mutant penguin forged from such a union would look like. Would it have the Emperor's beak or the King's? Would its body be short like the King's or tall like the Emperor's, or would it be some height between the two?

And would its waddle resemble the one or would it resemble the other? And all of these conjectures came to a head when all three of the Old King's daughters laid eggs not in the hatchery but in their massive home and, miracle upon miracle, The Greenmaker working in mysterious ways and all that jazz, the three eggs hatched into not mutants by their appearance but King penguin chicks.

Now how on ice did this happen? How did it come to pass? It could not be any of the sons who had fertilized those eggs since they had long since left on their journey. And then the questioning was narrowed down to the Old King himself. Surely he had not copulated and thereby fertilized his own daughters' eggs?! Surely he had not in one fell swoop become father and grandfather at the same time?!

Incest was not popular in the Emperors' colony. Incest was considered repugnant and taboo, both by Greenies and Penguanitarians alike. But how else could one explain three new King chicks coming on the scene when there were only three female adults and one male adult in the colony, the latter the father of the former? And so, the Old King had some explaining to do. Some very serious explaining to do. And despite his riches and his influence and his status as The Chosen Penguin, it was perhaps this state of affairs that would herald more so than any other hitherto his expulsion from the colony. And those impoverished penguins were rubbing their worn flippers together in glee, hoping upon hope that it would be found out that he had committed what was considered the most unnatural crime of all. But as per usual, the Old King was way ahead of them all.

#

Since relations between the Penguanitarians and the Greenies had become frayed of late, the former now making up the bulk of the colony, as much as eighty per cent thereof, and dominating completely The Council, the Old King knew he could once again put his duplicitous beak to good use, manufacturing two completely different accounts, both of which would be tailored to their respective faction.

#

To the Penguanitarians, he explained with great shame upon his face that not he of course but a rogue penguin had copulated with his daughters and thereby fertilized their eggs. *A rogue penguin?* they asked.

Oh yes. A rogue penguin. No, it wasn't any penguin from the colony that did the cheeky act but some outsider, the Old King informed them.

And how then could some rogue Emperor penguin, perhaps a loner or from one of the barbaric colonies out searching for prey and who had picked up on somehow that of the females being in heat, well, how could such a rogue Emperor copulate with a King female? And with all three of them at that?

The bodybird said it once again when pressed upon by the Penguanitarians that such a union was virtually impossible. And that was when the Old King laughed. Yes, he laughed as though he were mocking all of them for having thought such a thing, for having been so hasty in their thinking.

No, you see, explained the Old King, *it wasn't an Emperor penguin who had copulated with his three daughters and thereby fertilized their eggs but a Wakwak penguin.*

A Wakwak penguin? There was no such thing. They'd heard of Adélies and Rockhoppers and Macaronis. And they'd heard of Galapagos and Gentoo penguins. They'd even heard of a penguin called a Jackass. But a Wakwak? That was something new to them. They asked him to explain what exactly a Wakwak penguin was and what it looked like. And the Old King began answering before they had even finished posing that question to him:

The Wakwak, as it turned out, was a close relative of the King penguin. Even closer genetically than the Emperor was to the King. And Wakwaks were kind of like the dumb cousins. And although it would have been quite against all odds of a Wakwak at one go being able to copulate with all three and fertilize the eggs of all three as well, it was not altogether an impossible task either. Of course, the King lamented, the chicks, though they be my grandchicks all, will be somewhat retarded, for the Wakwak was considered one of the dumbest penguins ever known. In fact, it always amazed the Old King, who had come across numerous Wakwaks in his many travels, that there were any of them left at all by now. He then went on to explain that in the King penguin language back when there were enough of them to speak it, he now being the only official depository of that ancient tongue, well, in that language of his there had been an old saying. And it went like this: the Wakwak always swims towards the orca. Yes, that was how dumb the Wakwak was. And really, the Old King went on to conclude before waddling off, it was amazing that the King penguin was more or less extinct while the silly little Wakwak was still to be found here and there.

When the Penguanitarians turned to the bodybird and asked him if he'd ever heard or seen a Wakwak penguin, the bodybird shook his head. But at the same time, he said, there could well be Wakwak penguins out there somewhere. Indeed, he and the other penguins in the colony were not as well-travelled as the Old King. And since the Emperors more or less had never really left Antarctica or even sub-Antarctica, who was to know all the different species and subspecies of penguin that were out there.

#

Now for the Greenies, the Old King had to embellish a much more poetic tale. And if telling them of prophetic dreams had worked over and over again in the past, then it was sure to work just as well now.

And so, invited into the Greenie Monument, his beady black eyes covetously watching The Sacred Greenstone as he spoke, the Old King told them of the dream. And who do you think appeared in this dream of his but none other than The Greenmaker! Yes, no common or mortal penguin ever appeared in the Old King's dreams. And The Greenmaker had asked him if usury was helping, to which the Old King had replied that yes, that more and more penguins now had access to loans than ever before, and if necessary to loans for loans and loans for loans for loans. And with these loans they were able to feed their families and rent or even purchase igloos. And The Greenmaker had said that he was delighted to hear such good news. And he was delighted too that His Sacred Greenstone was back again now a long time where it was destined to be. And for having committed such magnificent acts for the colony, The Greenmaker had wished to bestow upon The Chosen Penguin that which he most desired in the world.

At this point, someone in the congregation hissed to the penguin next to him, "More gold!" and this set the whole line of penguins into fits of laughter. But the Old King continued his spiel.

What the Old King wished above all things, apart that is from the Greenies living in love and fraternity and out of the jaws of poverty and pain, was that his own subspecies could be saved, that his subspecies could somehow continue on The Greenmaker's white snow and ice. And that was when He had told the Old King that it would be done. That his daughters, all three, would soon come of age and would lay eggs. And that those eggs would have been fertilized by none other than He himself, The Greenmaker. And he was to tell the Greenies about this momentous occasion and get them to share with him all the joy of the world. His fertilizing the Old King's daughters' eggs would forever be celebrated and be called *The Stainless Fertilization*. And because of it, not only would these chicks be The Chosen Chicks, but on their coming of age they would have the status of half-penguin half-deity beings.

Well if this announcement didn't cause a stir there and then in the Greenie Monument. While many cheered this great news and congratulated The Chosen Penguin on the hatching of his grandchicks, anointed grandchicks to boot, others swooned, so overcome with emotion were they. Only a rare few in the congregation didn't believe a word of what they were being told, but nobody, now caught up in the euphoria, was going to listen to a few jealous penguins, who only didn't believe The

Chosen Penguin's account because they, unlike The Chosen Penguin, had never been chosen by Him up there somewhere in the sky, now looking down upon them with love and tenderness and compassion.

#

And so, having given each faction a different account, from a rogue and hitherto unknown species of penguin called a Wakwak to three whole stainless fertilizations performed by none other than The Greenmaker Himself, The Old King's head was firmly off the chopping block and, for now, his family, his growing family, a dynasty, had the whole colony to tighten its grip on.

CHAPTER 23: PRIVATIZATION

What was his grand plan? some of the common penguins would often ask each other in the privacy of their igloos. What really was his plan? And if it was to control every aspect of the Emperors' colony, surely he knew that absolute control was never really absolute and would come back to peck him quite sharply in the rear end. Surely, the Old King, being so old and clever, was old and clever enough to know this. And yet, he seemed to be forever plotting and scheming and coming up with new ways to impoverish and enslave them.

Nonetheless, the time came for the Old King to spread his flippers. With the jewellers' thriving and with igloos being built left, right and centre, from which and along with those he already had, he was making a very large income indeed, he had at the same time begun buying up large heaps of food and stockpiling them in a new building close to his home. He knew that gold was only ever as valuable as it was believed to be by others but that food would never lose its total value, especially its being almost imperishable in this frozen landmass. And should the supply of food drop, he would have the most precious commodity of all to trade in and to consume at his own leisure as well.   He had not thought all this out into reasoned speech. In fact, it would be as fair to say that he had never even thought up of this the first time he had executed it long ago in a faraway place, an instinctual drive seemingly leading him to whatever scheme would best serve his subspecies and annihilate the need for physical labour for that same subspecies.

Introducing gold as a currency would benefit him and his subspecies because he had initially all of the gold reserves. Likewise when he was on Tierra del Fuego, it had been silver instead of gold. Either way, the system worked. And now, if he could acquire all the food and somehow lower the supply thereof, he could become yet more powerful. And to maintain that power, he simply had to get them to return to traditional barter when he had a mountain of food to trade, and thereafter to convince them once again to go back to gold, and so on, and so on. Once he could keep convincing them to change from food to gold and from gold to food, he could hold onto power and lord it high above all of them, and perhaps even each time as the system of commerce would change, his grip on power instead of just being maintained would grow tighter and tighter. And if things ever went awry, which was always a possibility, there was always that glacier there. And failing that, there would always be many, many more Emperor colonies here on Antarctica that go could enrich, or perhaps better said, become enriched by.

#

Now if there was one thing that got on the Old King's nerves, it was the colony system of allocating gold pieces to the workers as salaries, and even allocating gold pieces to the invalids and elderly, so that they could buy their provisions – and their provisions were made up chiefly of food, fuel, rent and, for those who could afford it, the occasional splurge in his jewellers'. And even though he and the members of The Council and the most successful building contractors were able to buy up tonnes of food for themselves every week, there was still enough fish gut and fish head and scales and tails and bones left over for even the lowliest of penguins in the colony. No matter how much he and his cronies bought up the food from the Food Wareigloo, more food would come in. Ergo, for the Old King, the problem with the system was that there was too much food coming in on a daily basis.

And so, he decided to speak with the members of The

Council at his home, to throw a most generous soiree for them so as to pick their brains on an idea he had had. And the idea was one word. It was a long word. A word that didn't easily role off the old beak. And that word was *privatization*

#

Privatization of the Food Wareigloo. Take it out of public flippers and put it into private ones, namely his and theirs and in the flippers too of some more upstanding citizens to tie up the consortium and give the whole turnover a more transparent look.

Now as greedy as the members in The Council were and as much as they wished to profit more, they felt that this was a waddle too; that if the common penguins got wind that public ownership of the food supply should fall into private flippers, there could well be a revolt, a revolt that would be impossible to put down.

And the Old King laughed at the naivety of their concerns. Like them, he believed in doing the penguane thing. And he explained to them that instead of sending his PA down to the Food Igloo the other week, he had made it his business to go down himself and see what was going on down there. And, he stated, the place had been a shambles. Everything had been in disarray. And there had been different queues for different foods. And he had noticed much to his horror and chagrin that many, many penguins could barely afford the very basics, that which was even less than offal. And it had broken his heart to see this. Here he was and here the members of The Council were and the successful building contractors were, all comfortable and without a fear of going hungry, whilst their comrades were becoming weak and were lacking energy due to a diet of rubbish, and such a diet that they could hardly afford to have as well.

The members of The Council asked him then what they should do, and also to explain more this concept of privatization. Well, if the Old King had up till now been speaking with a great deal of lamentation, he suddenly waxed jovial. Privatization, he explained, was a way to ensure that a place or business was tobogganed efficiently. You cut off the excess, the wastage. You reduced costs and improved the product in terms of price and quality. If he and they could acquire the Food Wareigloo and could toboggan it between them, then that would mean that the whole colony could benefit. It would mean no more old widows bringing home nothing more than fishtails in their flippers but instead as good a food as the gentlepenguins like the Old King and his guests were consuming. Because hitherto, the problem, although some silly young penguins, troublemakers, had been bandying it about, was not due to the Old King and his cronies buying the choicest pieces of food in massive quantities, but was rather due to the Food Wareigloo being tobogganed badly, inefficiently, and therefore being tobogganed into the ice. If it could be tobogganed in a professional manner, food prices would drop and all would benefit. The Old King and his consortium would benefit, he claimed, not in a material sense but in a spiritual one, in a penguane one, because they would be helping to feed all the better all residents of the colony. And there could be nothing more penguane than helping to feed your brother-penguin. And furthermore, a full penguin was a healthy penguin, and a healthy penguin was a better worker. *And*, one of the members of The Council shouted out, *penguins who spend less money on food will have more money to spend on rent.* And all laughed. And then one of the building contractors said that less money spent on food would mean more money being spend on the construction of more igloos. And all laughed again.

    Flippers were extended. And flippers were shaken. And this time there would be no meeting held. No. It was decided that the average penguin did not need to know about this takeover since the average penguin, the poor thing, the common penguin, lacked both the sense and intelligence to know what was good for him...or her.

CHAPTER 24: LET THEM HAVE SCALES!

At first the new takeover did not cause any real changes. All it meant was that members of The Council could be seen there at the Food Wareigloo for the first time in months, and without a PA anywhere near them as well. And then the Old King would spend a few hours there in the evenings, waddling along from section to section on his waddling stick, speaking kindly to some of the penguins waiting in line to pay for their food, now and then offering a few gold pieces to the widows and their little chicks. He told them that he and the other Penguanitarians had found out to their utter horror that most of the penguins were not getting their proper food. And all those penguins in line shouted out in unison that that was true, that it had been thus for a long, long time. And the Old King assured them that from now on, with a few dye-in-the-plume Penguanitarians like him at the helm, things were going to change around here. Things were going to get better. The most succulent squid would be on their table within days. No more fishtails. No more scales. And no more fish guts. And on hearing this, many of the penguins waiting in line cheered and offered him their thanks. Maybe, they thought, as the Old King waddled off to another queue of downtrodden penguins, maybe he wasn't so bad after all. And some Greenies there in the queues thought that despite their referring to him of late as The Anti-Greenmaker, well, maybe, he was The Chosen Penguin after all, brought here by destiny to improve their lot down here on ice.

#

Likewise did both the Old King and his consortium spend time out on the ice with the netters, watching how they set their nets and how they retrieved them, timing the digging, measuring the depth of ice each time with a length of driftwood, which was the standard unit of measurement. And they spoke to the netters too, asking them about their jobs and how things around here could be improved both for them and for that of increasing fish stocks. And although the netters were suspicious of these penguins shadowing them throughout the day, they soon began to trust them, feeling sure now that they really were here just to find out how to improve things for all. And the netters became very forthcoming, many of whom not realizing that the more they explained things, the more they offered sound advice on how to increase yields, the more likely it was that they would soon be out of a job.

#

First and foremost, it was agreed amongst the consortium that for a whole fortnight they would not buy any food themselves from the Food Wareigloo, instead, living off of their stockpiles – that way, the best food would be available to all and all would think that the privatization scheme really was for their betterment.

Females were queuing up, paying with their usual meagre supply of gold pieces and leaving the joint with a massive flipperful of squid or krill or fish, as succulent and juicy as it had been in the days of yore, before gold has become the mandatory currency of trade. *It is amazing,* they said. *The Penguanitarians have taken over and already they have turned things around. Now our stomachs will no longer be aching and keeping us from a good night's sleep. It is just a pity they didn't take over the old place ages ago. But as the saying goes:* better late than never. And for two weeks all penguins in the colony were in buoyant mood, were healthy and satisfied with their lot in life. And then came the changes. Big changes.

#

There was too much food coming into the colony on most days. Ever since nets had been devised and utilized, there had always been a massive food supply, even on days when the catch was small, since the Food Wareigloo had always stockpiled mounds of it. It was really only when the gold system started that food, though in reality as plentiful as ever, became scarce for those at the bottom of society, it being bought up by wealthy penguins, leaving the those penguins at the bottom to food that was really waste and not a whit nutritious.

And now, as the consortium had control over food production, and once the populace had been lulled into a false sense of security, the Old King and the biggest stakeholders in the consortium began in earnest ringing in changes whose ramifications would be huge and devastating, well, devastating for all except them.

#

There were way too many workers, they said. And too many cooks spoil the broth. Half of the staff in the Food Wareigloo were made redundant, their redundancy packages being very paltry indeed. Next, seventy percent of the netters were given their marching orders. Those netters who remained were no longer to set the industrial-sized nets but nets that were much, much smaller. Smaller nets, obviously, would catch less food. And not only that, less nets overall were to be set. Those netters who remained scratched the plumes atop their head:

How could they maintain or increase fish yields by using smaller nets and less nets withal?

Whatever shortcomings there were in the food supply with these changes were offset by using up the surplus in the Food Wareigloo's stockpiles. And so, although barely a few morsels of food were being brought into the colony each day by the netters, nobody was any the wiser, the food supply and prices remaining unchanged and generous. The honeymoon period could not last, however, and was about to come to an end. And things would not be helped by the netters, who had been made to work extra-long shifts, taking it upon themselves to throw up their nets and to go on strike.

#

It came to everyone's surprise to see every single igloo in the colony that belonged to the Old King and the richest Penguanitarians suddenly going up for sale. Of course, nobody could understand why. Perhaps, some of the poor Penguanitarians claimed, clinging to the tenets of their creed, perhaps the Old King and those rich Penguanitarians wanted to give back to the community since all seemed so rosy in the garden, since everyone had enough food. And maybe by selling their igloos, they were trying to make the way clear for some young penguins to get their feet on the property ladder and climb out of the rental game. Whatever motives the penguins considered, they presumed all had to be from penguane motives. To be sure, the Old King and the Penguanitarians had made everything better. Whatever they seemed to touch made everything better. Take the Food Wareigloo for example: that place had been recently a disaster zone and there had been for a long time only scraps for penguins, and then these great Penguanitarians took over and suddenly the whole colony had more food than it could gulp down or regurgitate to others.

But unbeknownst to many of the common penguins, the word not reaching them or their not caring to listen to the plight of others, the netters had been on strike for a whole week already. And also unbeknownst to the common penguins was the fact that the stockpiles in the Food Wareigloo, which had been added to over many, many seasons as part of the Emperors' forward planning and contingency, were now depleted. On hearing about all this, the consortium convinced the netters to return to their posts with promises of less working hours and increased pay. And the netters, after much deliberation, returned. But despite the precarious position the colony was in, the netters were told to use the same small nets.

#

And then suddenly on one day, a penguin could only purchase with the same gold pieces as usual half the amount of food. And when the penguins, deeply dismayed by this sudden reduction of food, asked what was going on, they were told that pickings from the sea had been slim of late. And so, the penguins asked if the Penguanitarian consortium could not do what had been done before when the place had been a public institution, could they not dip into the stockpiles. And this was where they were told that that is exactly what the consortium had been doing the last number of weeks.

Furthermore, they were told that pickings at sea had been meagre for months, but somehow the consortium, in their great penguaneness, had pulled out all the stops to feed the entire colony. Oh yes, the consortium had gone above and beyond the call of duty, the Old King and the members of The Council coughing up their own gold pieces so as to feed the colony, and who now were as poor as everyone else. Of course, this last statement was not believed by a good number of residents, but they did not say anything to the contrary. And on the following day, the same gold pieces could no longer purchase half the quantity of food but a quarter thereof.

#

Starvation became rampant across the colony. And still, the food being brought in every day seemed to dwindle. And apart from the odd tip from one of the netters, very few knew about the new system of fishing. Very few knew about the fact that less and less nets were being set down beneath the ice. And much smaller nets as well. They were told that the sea just wasn't providing sustenance these days. Perhaps due to fish stocks migrating. Some season or climatic reason. Or perhaps, the Greenies themselves thought, perhaps The Greenmaker was angry with them again, this time for having erred away from Him and His teachings. Chicks, a mere two or three days out of the egg, perished, their parents, despite all their attempts, not being able to regurgitate anything for them. And, as was the custom for unhatched eggs or dead chicks, or dead adults for that matter, they were lowered into the sea after a much revered and lengthy sermon, whether the deceased were a Greenie or a Penguanitarian. There would be many such ceremonies carried out over the next weeks as the famine took hold.

#

And so, desperate times called for desperate measures. Meetings were held nightly to give the latest updates about the sea under the ice and the co-ordinates of this shoal and that shoal and how soon the nets would be bursting at the seams once again; how a storm that had been raging out at sea for weeks may have been the reason for so little in the way of their food supplies.

Of course both the Old King and the members of the Council were unwilling to attend these meetings lest they be lynched by the mob. One member's PA, who had been chairing one of these meetings was literally pecked to pieces by five hungry male penguins, the latter all being thrown into the cage that night and now awaiting trial. Rumours were starting to circulate too about the Old King's home outside the colony and how he had his very own stockpile of food. A mountain of food, they said. And as the hunger grew, the rumour did too. And the Old King with his many eyes and beaks on the ice, heard the rumour in no time at all and quadrupled his security team, all of which happened to be very well fed, as were his plump daughters and grandchicks/chicks.

#

An emergency meeting was held in the Old King's home one evening between him and the consortium, some of whose members had shown up with bloody beaks, having been accosted and assaulted by starving penguins. Something would have to be done. And it would have to be done without delay. The cages were full. They could not arrest any more rebellious penguins without such an action leading to outright revolution and revolt. If the food supply were not increased within the next couple of days, the colony would be lost, and with it all in attendance now would lose their lives.

The Old King had been expecting this turn of events. He had not mentioned any of this to them of course, but he had been expecting it. That was why he had sold his igloos: he knew there would be no rent received when there was no food. He knew the colony's economy would be on the ropes once he had control over their food supply. The fact that some of the rich Penguanitarians had also sold their igloos was not due to anything of which the Old King had informed them – rather it was down to them copying everything he did because they knew he was very smart, so much smarter than they. And if he did something, there was sure to be profit in it. And so they themselves would do likewise.

And the consortium members standing around in a circle in the Old King's massive igloo were surprised at how calm and stoical he was when compared to them. And he said to them matter-of-factly that the food supply would be ramped up on the morrow. He cleared his throat and said the following to them without having to catch his breath once. *Go out to the igloos and recruit the old netters, the ones that were laid off. And if some of them are in cages, then set them free and to work. And for the rest of them in the cell, expel them straight away from the colony. They may well be tainted with you-know-what: Barbarian-reversion – and that, as I have explained umpteen times, must be eradicated from the colony as soon as it rears its ugly head. Take the large industrial nets out of storage and have them ready for the morning. Allay their fears. Allay the common penguins' fear. Tell them anything that they want to hear. Remember, the important thing above all others is that we ameliorate the living conditions for all the common penguins as soon as possible. It is the penguane thing to do. And what is penguane is good for the colony. Otherwise, our beloved colony will be ripe for the taking. Yes, ripe for the virus of Barbarian-reversion. And we can't have that. No, we can't have our beloved and tolerant colony beset by Barbarian-reversion. And ensure you tell the common penguins that you have heard accounts, corroborated of course, of an enormous flock of seagulls some miles off in one of the icefields, and that where there are seagulls there is food, lots and lots of food.*

And the consortium left, their spirits raised once again: for if he told them how to remedy the situation, how to stem revolt, then revolt would be stemmed and they could continue thriving off the sweat and blood of their brother-penguins.

#

All of the industrial nets were set early the next morning, covering huge swathes of the sea beneath the ice. And by that evening, net after net was hauled up and transported into the centre of the colony and thence to the Food Wareigloo. And as an act of kindness and penguaneness, the food would be given away for free to feed the starving masses. And all cheered and took as much as they could carry back to their igloos.

Quickly was it announced that that night, on seeing that the seas were once again providing them with enough food on which to live, a party was organized. All penguins were invited to attend. It was a party to mark the end of hardship and the beginning of prosperity once again in the colony. And the guest of honour for the party, who had once again been able to turn things around for the betterment of all, would be none other than The Chosen Penguin, or, as they were beginning to call him of late in the social circles of the Penguanitarians, *Doctor Penguanity*.

#

After a fortnight of normal food production having been resumed, the Old King sold his share in the consortium to the other members, selling it for quite the profit too. And he ensured that his messengers spread word about the colony that the Old King, having improved things for them was now no longer in anyway connected to their food supply. And so, if prices were to shoot straight back up and if most of the penguins yet again would only be able to acquire scales and fish heads and fish guts and fishtails, then that would have nothing to do with The Chosen Penguin. No, no, they would then have to direct their wrath at the consortium and not at him.

And prices of course would shoot back up. And food scraps would be the diet in the colony for a great majority of the penguins yet again. And the Old King's penguanal stockpile of food would grow so large that he would have to start another stockpile, and for that he would have to get another igloo built in which to store it.

CHAPTER 25: HATCHING A NEW PLAN

Now no sooner had the Old King relinquished his stake in the Food Wareigloo than he set his beady black eyes on another prize. And that was the hatchery. In fact, unbeknownst to the wider public, part of the deal of the Old King selling his stake to the rest of the consortium was that The Council would privatize the hatchery and open bidding to the public. Of course the bidding was a farce. The bidding was done merely to feign transparency, the Old King already having been given the keys to the place.

The penguins could not understand why the hatchery needed to be privatized in the first place. It was simply a large igloo for eggs. All females went there and laid their eggs. Rows and rows of eggs were kept near a warm roaring fire, and there were three such fires in the hatchery. Three broody old females tended these fires and cleaned the eggs every so often. Once there was fuel and once these females were at their posts, nothing really could go wrong.

#

Of course it was only the way of things for some eggs never to hatch. But nobody could blame anyone for that, could they? And of course, it was only the way of things for one of the old broody females to accidentally tread on an egg or two from time to time. But accidents do happen now and then, don't they?

And once in a blue moon, the layout for the eggs got muddled up and the hatchlings were sent to the wrong parents. But what one doesn't know doesn't upset one, right? And of course in any hatchery it could only be expected that a small percentage of those eggs would never hatch, would be duds – and if the parents happened to be Greenies, the other Greenies would put this down to His vengeance on them for having shirked from their duties to Him by not having attended all ceremonies hosted in the Greenie Monument.

And if the parents happened to be other than Greenies, the other residents of the colony would jeer at the male involved and say that he was shooting blanks, much to his anger it must be said: for no greater an insult was there for an Emperor male's honour than it being bandied about in a colony that he was unable to reproduce. Indeed, often great duels would break out over this insult and deaths therefrom were not altogether a rare occurrence.

#

Now to convince the colony that The Chosen Penguin's acquisition of the hatchery was just another one of his penguane projects, just like that of the food supply, which under his stewardship had improved and worsened and improved, and then with his exiting from it had worsened yet again, he convoked one evening a monster meeting.

Here, he brought to light some hitherto unknown information on the hatchery and its management, or, better said, mismanagement. The three broody old females, whom he declared must be congratulated for their years of hard work and who had helped bring so many new lives into the colony, were now no longer the fit young birds they had once been. And therefore, if one could just throw off the sentimental blinkers for a moment, one would see that new blood was needed, more energetic blood, to increase the hatchery's success: for the future of the hatchery was key. *A colony that cannot breed has no future* went one of the oldest of all refrains.

And then, to prove that there was vindication in his proposal to making redundant the three old broody females, the Old King suddenly presented to the crowd a rotten egg. He held it up high in his flipper so that the sight of it would reach all of them. Of course, the three old broody females who were there in attendance and were by now feeling mortified, could not remember any such egg having been in their possession, but they were afraid to voice this publicly since he was The Chosen Penguin after all, and to take on The Chosen Penguin in front of others, a penguin who unlike them was so learned and so well-travelled, would be social suicide. No, the females tacitly agreed that it'd be best to keep quiet and let him squawk.

And squawk he did. Still holding the rotten egg up for all to see, and smell if some there were capable of smelling it, The Old King started speculating. He started speculating on the life that could have hatched from this precious egg that was no in his flipper. Would it have been a male or a female? Would it have worked as a netter or labourer or contractor or in the Food Wareigloo? Would it have been a great thinker or have had much brawn and worked in security? Oh, there were ever so many probabilities when a chick was still in the egg. And nothing was predestined, apart that was from the Old King himself having been chosen by Him, and by Nurture too. And Nurture it would have been that would have helped shape this chick that did not survive. And the chick had not survived because of the old regime in the hatchery's incompetence and even, perhaps, dotage.

The females in the crowd all commenced braying and spitting salt. They had been calm and uninterested in this meeting until the Old King had presented them with this egg. And the egg had carried no real importance for them until he had started hypothesizing of the life that was never given a chance. Many angry beaks turned towards the three old broody females and all agreed that the Old King should bring in young blood to toboggan operations there. And having gained their acceptance of this motion, the Old King put the rotten egg down and nominated his own daughters to take over the tobogganing of the hatchery.

There was a silence. They couldn't understand why they were silent, but something about this did not seem right. His daughters tobogganing the hatchery? And then the members of The Council began applauding this news and nodding to each other. And the contagion of applause thence spread throughout the crowd. And because they were all applauding, they all became happy. All that is, except for the bodybird. And it was noticed by The Council and by the Old King that the he was not applauding.

#

The meeting having been a resounding success, the Old King stretching his flippers as if to signal all the plans he was now going to carry out, all the changes he was going to ring in, another meeting was called that same evening. And this meeting would not be attended by the Old King but by four members of The Council and someone else. And that someone else was summoned by decree. That fifth attendee was the bodybird. And right from the off he was told by them that this would just be a casual little chat, nothing too formal, a beak-to-beak when all was said and done.

The bodybird was informed that, well, it was noticed, and to use a double negative, it couldn't not be noticed, that his flippers at the meeting over the privatization of the hatchery and the Old King's taking it over so as to increase standards, and thereby productivity, yes, his flippers, it had been noticed, hadn't been applauding in sync with all of the other pairs of flippers there. And it now had to be put to the bodybird, who was an intelligent penguin, whose father before him had been an intelligent penguin too, and whose grandfather certainly was in no way a fool either, well, it had to be put to the bodybird as to why he did not applaud the good news. Had he not listened to what the Old King had said? Had he not listened to this part of the Old King's speech: a colony that cannot breed has no future? Or did the bodybird have some penguanal gripe against the Old King?

And if so, whence did this enmity come? And how best could it be resolved since all that the members of The Council wanted was for all penguins to live penguanely amongst each other and not squabble? And surely that was not too much to ask for?

The bodybird was not one to feel pressurized or intimidated by others. He had always called things as he saw them. And that was how he came to be very much respected in the colony. His gruffness could ruffle a few feathers of course, but overall he was well considered by most. Not only did he mend broken bones and offer physical advice, but, as has already been mentioned, he was also a sort of sage and was said to know a little bit about a hell of a lot. And now, surrounded by the eager heads of several members of The Council, all of whom the bodybird presumed were in the orbit of the Old King, the bodybird nonetheless spoke his mind.

He explained to them in the simplest terms possible that a hatchery should never be privatized: *There should never be a private interest in something that is for the public good, the public good in this case being the prerequisite for any colony if it were to at least be maintained in terms of population but which would be hoped and expected to grow and to prosper*. What was good for the goose was not always good for the gander. He himself had been against the privatization of the Food Wareigloo and had said as much, but nobody would listen. And now, those members of The Council, who were having this beak-a-beak with him, were not serving the social weal but rather their own collective greed – hearing this, both shocked and angered the members: they had not realized that the bodybird, whose opinion counted, had such a low one of them. But being ever diplomatic, the members brought the bodybird back to the business of the hatchery and the Old King. Apart from all his talk of public good and prerequisites, just what was his burning issue with the hatchery?

Well, never had the bodybird been seen becoming so impassioned over anything. Never! No matter how stressful the situation, he had always seemed to keep his head. Many said he was somewhat detached from things even though he would be physically immersed in them. But in regard to the privatization of the hatchery, his plumes suddenly seemed to become erect as though charged by an electrical current. And he said that as bad as it was for the hatchery to be privatized, the fact that it was being flippered over to a different subspecies altogether spoke volumes. Spoke so many volumes that it was deafening. How could a penguin who was not an Emperor be put in charge of safeguarding Emperor eggs and hatchlings? How could this come about? It was unnatural. Yes, it was certainly not the natural order of things.

    A subspecies' aim in life, the bodybird lectured them, was to replace another subspecies if it so happened that they were in the exact same biosphere. The bodybird did not deem this to be malevolent or some sort of hidden demon but rather the workings of the natural word itself. Just like the tide coming in and then going back out. But the idea of putting the future of the colony squarely in the flippers of a different subspecies would mean the death of the former and growth of the other. It really was a no-brainer. And to hammer home the point, and knowing that one of the member's female was soon going to be laying an egg, he asked that member if his partner was going to lay that egg in the hatchery or at his own home where he had two broody old nannies of his own and had even recently hired his own private egg-matron. And inwardly gushing and much angered by such a question, the member said without stammering his words that of course he would be getting his partner to lay their egg in the hatchery. And why on ice would she lay it in their home? And the bodybird continued on this member's case by asking him then why he had recently employed an egg-matron then for his home if his partner was going to lay their egg in the hatchery anyway. And the member got very much flustered this time around and started spitting salt, and he said that his partner would lay her egg in the hatchery as all females did and would go on doing until the end of time, and that whether a King penguin or an Emperor penguin were calling the shots in the hatchery didn't make the least bit of difference because all were penguins. All were penguane creatures. And this member could see now that the bodybird was becoming like those they had expelled all those seasons ago. Yes, the bodybird reminded him by his way of talking and his stubbornness when it came to Nurture and Progress, reminded him very much it had to be said, of those who could not be mentioned: The Elders of Instinct.

And then all members there at the meeting asked the bodybird if it was true. Was what true? Was he a member or had he been a member of the Elders of Instinct? And the bodybird told them that he had never been a member of anything or anyone. That all he did was mend bones and offer sound physical advice. But the members kept up the ante. It seemed somewhat rehearsed, but they kept asking him over and over again to confess his membership. If he did not fess up now, things could get very, very bad for him indeed. And for his partner too. And his chicks. And even his cherished grandchick. Oh yes, things could get very bad for him unless he confessed.

And instead of confessing or pretending to confess, the bodybird laughed and left the meeting, waddling off in the direction of his igloo. But no sooner had he gone half way thither than he was set upon by a few big burly penguins and dragged off to the cage. The first obstacle against the privatization of the hatchery was now firmly out of the way.

CHAPTER 26: A WEE RENDEZVOUS

The Old King had a meeting of his own to attend the following morning. But it was not to be held in the colony or even in the comfort of his lush residential complex. And it was not one to be convened in the presence of penguins either. No, this meeting was a secret one and was to be held on the shingle beach, a place that very few penguins visited, even the netters, who were a tad superstitious and gave it a wide berth too. And there did the Old King alone meet his associates: a flock of skuas.

Now before the Emperors had begun building igloos and had discovered fire and had fashioned spears and nets, the skua had been their eternal enemy. No chick had ever been safe from their sharp beaks. No untended egg out on the ice would have been there for long either. And with skuas flying about or grounded on the outskirts of a colony, no penguin could be at ease. In fact, there was a common saying from those times: *around skuas never relax.*

What could bring the Old King hither then to communicate with such a flock of scoundrels? And why would he risk such a meeting? If he were caught here, here with the traditional enemy, then surely he would be expelled from the Emperor colony for once and for all. And with him his daughters and grandchicks/chicks.

Well, truth be told, business had brought him hither. And likewise business had brought the flock of skuas. The Old King now had access to things that the skuas longed for. And the skuas, being able to fly, would be able to acquire things that the Old King longed for. Ever the polyglot, he spoke their language and spoke it well. Quantities would have to be haggled over. But both parties knew that the agreement would be made no matter what.

The skuas would bring to the Old King something immaterial, namely, information. Information on the constant whereabouts of his sons. Information on the numbers of this penguin colony and that penguin colony. Information on leopard seals. And furthermore, with this regular briefing on what was going on all over the sub-Antarctic region, the Old King could be kept abreast of all the movements thereof, for the world to him was one big chessboard, its pieces constantly in flux, constantly useful and then surplus to requirements, or even becoming a liability.

And for this plethora of information that would be incoming at regular intervals, and which included correspondence between the Old King and his three sons, the skuas had to receive payment. And what would the Old King recompense them with for services rendered? Eggs. Emperor eggs. All the eggs they could devour if they were giving him reliable information. Unfertilized eggs at first. But, if the skuas showed themselves to be worthy business partners, they would even get the occasional fertilized egg thrown into the bargain. And, if they really worked hard, if they really covered the wide area in all sorts of dangerous weather, well, then the Old King would throw them a live chick or two. The skuas' eyes turned ravenous on hearing this. It had been so long since they had been able to gobble up an Emperor penguin chick. In fact, some of them had grown up without ever having tasted either Emperor penguin egg, recent hatchling or chubby chick.

The meeting adjourned, off flew the skuas to begin their reconnaissance missions. And off up to the top of the large glacier waddled the Old King, checking out the fissures that had widened since his last visit and calculating how much time he would have left on this continent if need be. He tobogganed down off the glacier and back onto the shingle beach and thence waddled off in the direction of the colony. He had a busy day ahead of him at the hatchery and many great changes in policy to make there.

CHAPTER 27: FEMALE LIBERATION OF EGGCELLENCE

The daughters of the Old King with permission from The Council began conducting classes, mandatory classes for all young female penguins who were coming of age. In these classes, that no male could attend or even eavesdrop on, the females were told time and time again that eggs were a sign of slavery and oppression – *their* slavery and *their* oppression that was. The egg, the daughters explained, was rejected by the body because it was not part of the body and was a waste product thereof. No egg was nice but the least terrible egg, they were told, was that which was unfertilized. An unfertilized egg meant liberty thereafter for the female. She could continue working her way up in her job and/or just kicking back and enjoying life. Because the essence of life, the Old King's daughters explained, was to enjoy it. To enjoy it at all costs. Carpe diem. Seize the day because tomorrow did not exist. And what did not exist could never be guaranteed. And what could not be guaranteed was not worth knowing at all at all.

The fertilized egg, however, meant a continued slavery for those females, for, that egg having hatched, they would have to feed around the clock a creature that did not resemble any penguin, a creature that depended on them for all its needs and thereby was enslaving them. To this statement from the Old King's daughters, one female in the class, a very conservative Greenie, raised a flipper and asked if she could bring up something that might be worth considering. The Old King's daughters, unsure of how to respond to this unorthodoxy – a student speaking instead of listening? – nodded their heads. And the female rather shyly stood up and started to explain to both teachers and classmates how Emperor penguins shared the duties of chick-rearing almost equally, especially if the male was not working long shifts as a netter or labourer, and how back in the day, pre-history, pre-igloo, pre-fire, it was known that it was the males who had incubated the eggs while the females had been free to go on long sea journeys and to bring back the food. The Old King's daughters nodded their heads again and said that this story was very interesting and thanked the female for sharing it with them and with the students. But that female was not welcomed back to class the next day.

The Old King's daughters explained how the hatchery had been a place of oppression up until now. Oppression for all females. Indeed, it was thither that females were led by their partners, the females themselves not having gone of their own free will, to lay an egg. And the egg was almost always the worst type of egg: a fertilized one. And the creature that would hatch from the egg was a horrible sight to behold. How could anyone in their right mind call that creature a penguin?! No, it was not a penguin. It was the wicked symbol of *their* oppression. That creature that had hatched from the egg was what would keep them from enjoying life and living it up. And so, that creature had to be squashed. It had to be "liquidated". And if the egg that bore it could be liquidated as soon as it was laid, then all the better: for then one would not need to witness the oppressive creature itself that smashed its way from that egg and needed feeding, that creature that – it had to be stated again – was not a little penguin at all but rather was a symbol of *their* female slavery.

Most of the female students nodded their heads in agreement when hearing this. And since the Old King's daughters were the richest females in the colony, that meant they were the most successful too. And being successful meant higher social status. And so, if the Old King's daughters, The Chosen Penguin's daughters, Doctor Penguanity's daughters, were telling them that eggs were evil, then evil they had surely to be. And the fact that the female students' existing here and now was due to their mothers laying fertilized eggs and rearing those hatchlings to adulthood didn't even seem to come into the equation for them at all. And even though it was known that the Old King's daughters all had chicks of their own, that they too had laid fertilized eggs and were now mothers to those chicks, the female students were either unable to grasp or even notice this glaring inconsistency or outright hypocrisy. And the mantra became simplified and all females were made to repeat it in unison and to sway side to side as they were doing so: *eggs are bad; fertilized eggs are worse; and all hatchlings are oppression itself.*

#

Now how would murder, embryocide or just downright slaughter of fertilized eggs be categorized in the Emperor colony? The word chosen would have to be a clever one, one which would ghost under the radar of contemporary morality. *Ejection* was considered at first. *Reproductive health* was considered too. *Shell-shock treatment* had been on the table for a while. *Liquidation* had been used frequently at the start as well. But in the end, The Old King and a few members of The Council settled on that which they considered to be the nicest, cleanest-sounding and softest-sounding word. They settled for the word *goo-goo*.

Yes, it sounded innocuous. The etymology was based on what a freshly-laid egg contained if opened up. And that was goo. Runny, sloppy, sludgy, messy, harmless old goo. The term quickly fell into common parlance and from there became defined equally as an adjective (*gooey-gooey*) and a verb (*to goo-goo*) and a phrasal verb (*to goo-goo in*) and an adverb (*gooely-gooely*).

And so, a female who had just come of age and did not want to spend her time rearing a chick, would, obviously if she had copulated with a male beforeflipper, *go for a goo-goo*. Likewise, she could tell other females whom she met on her way to the hatchery that she was about to *goo-goo in an egg*, namely to lay it and let the staff there destroy it at their leisure. In fact a female who was going to goo-goo in her egg was praised and embraced to no end by the other young females.

Henceforth was it agreed: females would have the right to choose whether to have their eggs fertilized or not. The only thing that was not an option in the process was to lay those eggs anywhere else but in the hatchery itself. And if a female were discovered laying an egg outside of the hatchery, she would have to pay a penalty for that crime. Because from now on it would be a crime.

To wit, going forward, whether fertilized or unfertilized, all eggs laid in the colony would go through the flippers of the Old King, and if not through his, then through those of his daughters.

CHAPTER 28: GREENIE REVOLT AGAINST GOO-GOO

When the Greenies got wind of these new changes, they hit the roof, well, if their place of worship had a roof, that is. How on ice could such a thing have come to pass? And how had they not been able to counter it sooner? They should have known that something was awry when The Council had implemented those classes for all females coming of age, and made those classes mandatory as well. And they should have reacted when the law was passed that gave females rights to have their eggs fertilized or not. Now The Council was going to let the females decide not only on whether an egg could be fertilized or not but whether a fertilized egg could reach its maturity to hatch or whether it would be terminated beforeflipper.

Much ruffled, they gathered in the Greenie Monument and tried to come up with a strategy that would end goo-goo, all goo-goos before they had really begun in earnest. Some said that they should go to the hatchery right now and demolish the building. Others said doing such a thing would mean reprisals from the Penguanitarians who were four or five times as numerous in the colony now as the Greenies. No, demolishing the hatchery would be suicide. They would have to think of other means.

A cleric who was on the rise in the Order whispered, knowing that to utter such words could mean the cage for him or worse, and sensing that there was a spy in their midst as well, but he whispered that maybe they should do away with the Old King, for no doubt his flipper seemed to be behind all that went wrong in the colony, and how it seemed as more and more time passed that he was in fact a manifestation of The Anti-Greenmaker. Well, this bold cleric was quickly cut short by the other clerics there.

Did this bold cleric not know that the Old King was not The Anti-Greenmaker but The Chosen Penguin? That to do away with him would surely enact The Greenmaker's wrath upon them all. And furthermore, was it not the Old King who had helped to improve food production and on whose leaving the consortium had caused the food prices to go back up, which could only signify that the Old King was more a benevolent being than a malevolent one. And furthermore, he was after all the grandfather to three penguin-deities whose father was none other than The Greenmaker Himself. And The Stonekeeper who stood in the middle of the congregation reminded the bold cleric and the rest that it was the Old King, The Chosen Penguin, who had recovered for them The Sacred Greenstone, which he now had in his flipper, and thereby had the Old King, The Chosen Penguin, redeemed them all.

No, The Chosen Penguin could not be harmed by any circumstances, natural or unnatural. Some other means would have to be used to stop goo-goo. And then an idea was pitched. How about demonstrating outside the hatchery? How about standing there and letting all passers-by know that goo-goo was a word that was really dripping in blood and wickedness. Goo-goo was an act that should not only rankle Greenies but Penguanitarians too since they believed in Penguanity and Nurture. And how was it Nurture when eggs would not be fertilized? And how was it Nurture if the eggs were fertilized but then the female could choose anyway to have the egg and chick inside crushed into a pulp? The male would have no rights whatsoever. It was murder. Murder pure and simple. And if the Penguanitarians wouldn't listen to that, surely they would understand that famous old refrain: *a colony that cannot breed has no future.*

#

The Greenies began their protest. They ensured that a dozen of them were standing outside the hatchery from dawn till dusk, squawking and squawking, letting the females know who were both entering and leaving the place, letting the Old King and his daughters know, that goo-goo was murder. And that The Greenmaker was firmly against murder. And that He would seek revenge on those who were facilitating this. And besides, how could laying unfertilized eggs or destroying fertilized ones, have anything to do with Nurture. In fact, goo-goo was the very opposite of that most esteemed tenet of Penguanitarianism. Yes, how could they look at themselves the next time they saw their reflection in water?!

However much they protested, business went on as normal at the hatchery. And despite illegally taking out many of the Greenie females from the mandatory classes, many more young females were enrolled still. And no sooner had these females been enrolled than they were out-and-out freedom-lovers, freedom-lovers who not only wanted to smash all eggs everywhere but all males too. The male, they were told, like that of the ugly-looking hatchling, wanted to chain them into slavery, wanted to fetter their feet and stop them from waddling out there into the great yonder, wanted to stop them from globewaddling and thereby finding their spiritual selves. And in lieu of eggs and hatchlings, the Old King's daughters told them that they could just as happily adopt a piece of gold from their father's jewellers', anything really once it was shiny and smooth to the touch. And the shiny thing, though it be inanimate and though they would care for it at their own leisure, would not attempt to enslave them as the male or hatchling would.

On the twelfth day of their protest, the Greenies there were set upon by a mob of henchpenguins, who beat them off with clubs and spears. And as the Greenies fled as if their lives depended on it, they were warned that if they returned to protest they would get more than a close shave the next time.

And so, the protests outside the hatchery ended. The Greenies, gathering together in the Greenie Monument brayed up to the sky, imploring Him to bring them salvation from such an evil that had beset their precious little colony. And although His green curtain of light would play across from horizon to horizon, there was no message conveyed back to them unless that message was meant to be mere silence. Consequently, with time passing and hopes fading, a sizable number of Greenies left the Order and joined the ranks of the Penguanitarians, forsaking the sky for the fruits of Progress, for whatever those fruits would in the end prove to be.

CHAPTER 29: CHICKICIDE & EGGSTRAVAGANCE

Now although his daughters had preached to all young females on how males and hatchlings were symbols of oppression, the Old King had known not to rush things along too swiftly. First and foremost, he had communicated via The Council, that only unfertilized eggs would be goo-gooed. And the Greenies had not publicly protested against this then because, even though they did not believe in the very notion of any egg being intentionally unfertilized, they were willing to let this slide since no life was being terminated thereby. And on that very matter, they thought: *who could deny a female's right to have her egg fertilized or not?* And even many of the female Greenies believed in this premise. As the progressive slogan went: *my egg, my choice.*

And so with the males, both Penguanitarians and Greenies alike, out of the decision-making process, it could only go from there to the notion that if the female alone could decide whether the egg would be fertilized or not, by a similar logic could she also decide whether a fertilized egg could be allowed to reach the stage of hatching or not. And it was on this topic that the Greenies had rallied and begun their protests.

But now, with those pesky Greenies beaten into submission and no longer protesting outside his business, the Old King planned to go even further with what goo-goo would encapsulate. If the female could decide whether her egg would be fertilized or not, and if she could decide also whether a fertilized egg could be hatched or not, then so too could she decide whether the chick, weak and clinging to life in the cold air, had the right to live or not. Naturally enough, the Old King was not going to push this last piece of legislation onto the unsuspecting public, not yet anyway. No, it was too early. They had not progressed enough in his mind to accept this. They, the bumpkins that they were, would call it chickicide no doubt, while he and his associates would call it, a panache of scientific jargon attached thereto: *Stage 3 goo-goo*.

Nonetheless, getting them to even consider such a thing as an unfertilized egg had been a great start for him. And now, having females, the overwhelming majority thereof, opting to have their eggs, both unfertilized and fertilized, goo-gooed, really had been a social revolution, a wonderful social revolution. It meant that the Emperor colony was on the wane. It meant that very soon, if not already, they would no longer be able to maintain their numbers, never mind be able to grow their current population. And a colony whose native species or subspecies was on the wane was a colony that would be open to all sorts of new experiments.

#

To drive home the point to the Greenies, to humiliate and demoralize them still further, to not give them time to lick their wounds and redouble their efforts against his business, the Old King's daughters arranged, with assistance from several members of The Council and many Penguanitarians, *The Eggstravagant Protest*.

In this simple act, a few dozen females, each one with an egg in her flipper, her own egg, waited patiently and excitedly on a day of service outside the Greenie Monument. When members of the congregation were filing out, the eggs were hurled at them. Some missed their target and smashed off the icy walls of the Greenie Monument, but others hit the Greenies square on the beak or right in the eye. One protester there threw an egg and when it smashed against the wall of the Greenie Monument, it was to be noticed that within it was a chick, bald as a coot and shivering for seconds before it froze and perished. And as soon as the dead chick was noticed by the female protesters, they waddled over to it and stomped the little carcass into the snow with their feet under a chorus of *Freedom* and *Love Not Eggs* and *Female Penguins Unite* and *No More Chains No More Misogyny*.

To say that the Greenie congregation wasn't shocked and appalled would be an understatement. Indeed, many of them seized the protesters and gave them quite the drubbing. If it were not for a number of Penguanitarian males showing up and dragging the females away, deaths of more than that single chick would no doubt have ensued.

#

The females who laid their unfertilized eggs in the hatchery were compensated with a shiny stone and a rare fish delicacy. If on the other flipper the female was laying a fertilized egg but stated that she opted to have it goo-gooed in, then she was rewarded with two shiny stones and two fish delicacies. And so, the hatchery, instead of becoming a beacon of life became a building of death.

Of course there were penguins who still went there like they had before to lay a fertilized egg, and who trusted the staff there to tend to it and bring a little joyous chick into their lives; however, the parents of such eggs and chicks many a time were told that the egg had failed to hatch or the chick had hatched and died instantly despite the staff doing all they could to save it. And when the unfortunate parents of these eggs or chicks called around to the hatchery to collect the remains so as to bring them to the sea and perform the traditional service of mourning, they were usually given some excuse or other for the remains having disappeared from right under the staff's beaks.

If there had been a statistician keeping record, he would have noted that in one breeding season in the colony, of five thousand eggs laid, most of which had been unfertilized, only twenty made it to be sturdy chicks. And of these twenty chicks, four of them had hatched in the hatchery itself; eight of them were the chicks of members of The Council, who strangely enough had flouted the law and laid their eggs in their own homes and not in the hatchery. Of the remaining eight, all had been laid secretly by rebellious Greenies, who knew that the hatchery was unsafe despite promises and re-utterances that the chief operator there was none other than The Chosen Penguin, a disciple of The Greenmaker Himself, He who loved life and reproduction and shared with them His green curtain of light – indeed, when it came to reproduction, these Greenies had been willing to dispel their faith entirely, rearing the chicks in secret and then sneaking them out of the colony at night, never again to return, their legacy leaving a bitter taste in the residents' beaks: *deserters!*

CHAPTER 30: BIRDS OF PREY

One morning, very early, before even the netters had risen and set off to their jobs, the Old King threw on some nesting, got a bag that was made from a seal's stomach and placed several items therein. He then headed outside. Little did he know that he was now being watched.

#

A young male Emperor, a Greenie true and true, had taken it upon himself to stake out the Old King's property. He had not informed anyone of his mission and he did not really have much in the way of a concrete plan. And had he been caught by the security team, he would not even have had the slightest excuse to present them with. But, having spent the night outside the high walls, atop which burned driftwood dipped in oil, and standing some distance away from the flickering light so as not to be easily seen, the young Greenie now watched with much eagerness the Old King himself pass by a few securitypenguins at the gates and waddle off not in the direction of the colony but in the opposite direction altogether.

#

It was a long waddle. The young Greenie made sure to keep well back. On one occasion the Old King stopped in his tracks and turned around. He looked in the direction of the young Greenie but did not seem to notice him and then turned back around and continued waddling. After quite some time the Old King reached the shingle beach. And the flock of skuas was there already waiting for him.

Now this was interesting for the young Greenie as he lay down flat on his belly and peered around a boulder. He had never seen a single skua in his life on terra firma: no, the only skuas he ever saw were those who flew over the colony at a very high altitude so as to be out of the range of the Emperors' spears. And here they were now perched on rocks and stones and waiting for the Old King to get down to where they were. And as the Old King neared them, the flock separated into two lines, as though giving him a guard of honour. Then they circled him and the young Greenie presumed that the Old King had made a serious blunder and that all the skuas were now going to go in for the kill and peck him clean. But strangely, this did not happen.

The Old King was squawking to the skuas and the skuas were squawking back. *How*, thought, the young Greenie, *does he know their language? And how can he squawk it so fluently at that?*

And the squawking went on for some time. And the young Greenie had not the faintest just what they were squawking about. Had he been able to understand, he would have found out that the Old King's three sons had bred with three King penguin females and were now families, and that they were slowly but surely making their way back to Antarctica and to the Emperor colony. Furthermore, had the young Greenie even a smidgeon of Skuaish, he would have found out that not only were the Old King's sons and daughters-in-law and grandchicks on their way back but that in tow was a number of Adélie penguins, and not dozens or score or hundreds but thousands of them. All males. No females.

When the Old King had finished a long squawk, all the skuas began flapping their wings and squawking in unison. It looked like they were suddenly very excited about something. So excited were they that they began jostling for position in front of the Old King and pecking each other. And then the Old King opened up his bag and took out an egg. The young Greenie squinted his little eyes as much as he could just so he could have no doubts about it. Yes, his eyes were not deceiving him.

THE CHOSEN PENGUIN

The egg that the Old King had taken out was that of an Emperor penguin.

And then the Old King threw the egg high up into the air and the skuas all immediately flapped and jumped, one of which actually took off in flight and caught the egg in its beak, the egg breaking and its contents tobogganing down to the hungry maze of beaks that tried to open to this sudden bounty. No sooner had the Old King thrown one egg than he threw another. And another. And another. And another. And another. And then, like a great magician about to perform his final trick, the Old King took out of his bag a chick, a live chick that was chirping and struggling against the flipper that held it.

No! screamed the young Greenie inwardly. *Please Greenmaker no! He's not...Please don't tell me he's going to...Oh Greenmaker!*

And the chick was dangled from the flipper and the largest of the skuas approached and the others hesitantly cleared the way for that skua. And the Old King tossed the live chick to the large skua. And in a flash the live chick was seized by the sharp beak. For a few seconds the chick's desperate chirping could be heard. And then in another flash, the large skua threw up his head and swallowed whole the live chick.

The young Greenie stuck his head back behind the boulder and squawked out in horror before cupping his beak with his flipper. Had they heard him? Surely they had heard him? And if they had, should he now try to make a break for it? But how far would he really get? The skuas could fly. They'd be upon him in no time. No, best to stay where he was and wait. Wait it out and hold tight. And after several seconds, which seemed interminable, the young Greenie decided that he should peer back out, just to see if the Old King and the skuas were still where they were, which would mean that they had not heard his squawk after all or had ignored it. But of course, what worried him now was that he did not hear any of them squawking over there. Unless that meant that the meeting had been adjourned and the skuas had taken to the air and the Old King was already

149

waddling back to his complex. The young Greenies waited and waited. Checking himself. Until he could wait no longer. And then he peered back around the boulder.

And oh what a mistake! The Old King and the skuas were still where they had been minutes ago down there on the shingle beach. But they were all staring in his direction. And this time it looked like the Old King had spotted him because he pointed a flipper in his direction and squawked what seemed like orders at the skuas. And the skuas took off in flight and made a straight line for him. There was nothing left to do. All the young Greenie could think of was to make a dash for it. And off he waddled. And within seconds he heard their squawking become shrill and piercing. And within more seconds he felt his little body being slapped by countless wings. And within even more seconds he felt the sharp sting of pain all over as their beaks began tearing his flesh to shreds. And within a minute his pains were becoming dull. And then came the cold. And then came the shivering against the cold. And then the dull colours seemed to fade and become even duller. And then the darkness came in from the peripheries of his vision. And then there was just sound. And after that, there was mere silence.

The young Greenie's carcass was stripped bare. And though he absolutely loathed manual labour, the Old King thought it best to cover his tracks when the skuas had gone. He dragged the carcass, which was as light as a feather, across the shingles and onto a low cliff and thence dumped it into the sea below. And as the Old King then waddled off back to his complex and then onto the hatchery to begin his day, the stones that were stained with blood were wiped clean by the incoming waves. And farther out a body bobbed and then something dragged it down to the depths below.

CHAPTER 31: DEMOGRAPHIC SHIFT & ADÉLIEPHOBIA

Life went on as normal or as abnormal as it had before. Gender quotas were agreed upon throughout the colony and to ensure that The Council would have as many females as males, twelve females, three of which were the Old King's daughters and the rest of which were young females who had gone through the full range of empowerment classes, were nominated into office. The business of netting, which had been carried out solely by males, was now to include half of its workers as females, although females found the task of digging through ice to set and haul out nets a very hard one indeed; in fact, it was said that the average female took twice as long to dig her way through the ice as did the average male, and with many males being laid off to make way for those females, the food supply was reduced by a significant amount. The hatchery continued receiving for the most part unfertilized eggs. The Old King's daughters continued teaching or indoctrinating the next class of females that were about to come of age. The members of The Council grew fat and were rarely seen in public and this, it was presumed, was so as not to be accosted by hungry and homeless penguins, of which there were many, and many more by the day. The Food Wareigloo, on account of female netters, brought in less food than it had hitherto. And now very little of it, including the leftovers even, made it to the common penguin's beak, the prices thereof being higher than ever. The Greenies' now-small congregation huddled within the four walls of the Greenie Monument at night and gazed up at His green curtain of light that played across from horizon to horizon and they beseeched Him for answers to their many problems, problems in regard to the lack of necessities that abounded them, both materially and morally. And the Old Penguin seemed throughout all of this, though tobogganing the show, to be more restless than he had ever been before. His secret visits to the shingle beach where he would meet the skuas became an almost morning routine. There was much astir. The Emperors were not to know, but there was much astir.

#

And then one evening, as night descended across Antarctica, the Emperors heard a great commotion of distant waddling and foreign braying. Whatever could it be? Was it another Emperor colony come to take over this one? A barbarous Emperor colony at that? Even though many of the Greenies whispered to each other that any barbarous invading colony could be no more barbarous than that of their own at this moment in time, a colony wherein the overwhelming majority of eggs were never fertilized, wherein fertilized eggs were smashed, and wherein even newly-hatched chicks were inpenguanely crushed to death with a small rock. No, the Greenies thought, as the waddling and foreign squawking drew nearer, whosoever was out there could only improve things by taking over this sorry state of affairs.

Many Emperors brandished their spears and lit torches, awaiting some sort of battle that would come out of the fading light. They waited and waited and waited. And then a familiar face came into the torchlights. It was one of the Old King's sons. And after him came the other two sons. And after them came three female King penguins with three King penguin chicks.

#

What had been thought of as being virtually extinct was now, with the hatching a while back of the Old King's daughters' three chicks and now with the appearance of the Old King's sons' three chicks , a species that was waddling back from the brink. And suddenly it was noticed by the few Emperors who were wont to notice such things that King penguin chicks made up a sizable percentage of young chicks in the colony.

Then came the Adélie penguins, waddling hesitantly forward. The Emperor penguins raised their spears once more. Taking in the Old King's sons and their wives and their chicks was one thing but to take in a couple thousand boisterous Adélie penguins was a completely different kettle of fish. The Adélies froze when the spears were raised and looked to the King penguin's sons to offer some assistance. And the King penguins quickly let the Emperors know that the Adélies were their friends, had helped them to no end on their journey to rescue the female King penguins who were now their wives, well, wives for this season anyway, since King penguins were not as monogamous as Emperors. And how could they, the Old King's sons not return the favour, the hospitality? How could they turn away such penguane brothers when they had helped to escort the last of the King penguin species here safely and soundly? And anyway, their stay would only be for the night since Adélies were not prone to live inland like the Emperors were, instead preferring to be on the coast among stones. But to this, the Emperors held their ground. They would not let them into the heart of the colony. Hospitality was one thing but letting two thousand hungry birds as these, all rowdy-looking males, into the colony could be a disaster. The numbers were far too high. If they wanted, they could wait out here and the Emperors would return with food and freshwater for them and if necessary some nesting to wear too.

The Old King's sons, who had already been swaddled in nesting to protect them from the cold, agreed publicly with the Emperors with the spears. But straight away, they made the long waddle to their father's complex. And there, the Old King came out with his sons, leaving the females and chicks behind to rest and to bond with his daughters and their chicks. The Old King called in on a member of The Council, who in turn called in on four other members. And in no time fifteen members of The Council and the Old King and the Old King's three sons were on the outskirts of the colony where stood the spear-brandishing Emperors and the two thousand noisy and boisterous Adélie penguins. Five Greenie clerics also hurried onto the scene, their flippers wide open to receive the newcomers.

The members of The Council did not waste much time before giving the Emperors on guard a right dressing down. How could they? How could they turn away fellow-penguins in need of a warm igloo? How could they turn away those penguane foreigners who had risked life and webbed foot in order to bring the Old King's own sons, Doctor Penguanity's own sons, all the way hither? Had they not learnt anything in the nursery when they were younger? Did the tenets of Penguanitarianism not mean diddlysquat to them? Oh there would be an investigation into this on the morrow. You could bet your life on that. A hell of an investigation. But right now all of them without exception were to lay down their spears and escort the poor Adélies into the colony and provision lodgings for them and ensure that all fires were lit. And that was an order. And though almost nobody was paying them any attention, the Greenie clerics began speaking about compassion and how compassion was part and parcel of His love up there in yonder night sky and how in His eyes a penguin in need, regardless of species, was a penguin of The Greenmaker and therefore could never be turned away: for turning away any penguin, regardless of species was in a way the exact same as turning away The Greenmaker Himself.

And the Emperors on guard laid down their spears. And they squawked at the Adélies to follow them, the latter not understanding what to them was a foreign tongue, and the former wondering where the hell they were going to accommodate such a number of penguins and why they even should since they had hundreds of their own iglooless and starving in the colony. And then with ease, the Old King intervened as interpreter and explained to all Adélies that they were to follow the guards back to the middle of the colony where they would all be able to rest in comfort and out of the elements. Well, the Adélies got very excited on hearing this. Sleeping indoors would be an absolute novelty for them. In their colony there were only stone whereon to stand. And now they were going to be sleeping between four walls with a roof on top. How peculiar! And how interesting!

With that, the guards waddled off, behind them two-thousand Adélies, who squawked up a terrible racket. And when all had gone off some distance, the Old King and his sons and the members of The Council exchanged a few words. And there did they all agree that many big changes would have to be made to accommodate the Adélie. And when they broached that topic, it seemed that they were expressing it in a way that was not short-term but long-term.

#

And the following day, the Adélies made no preparations to leave, which was strange for many of the Emperors who were loath to become acquainted with these new penguins. There was something about all of these Adélies that repulsed the Emperors. For starters they could not understand their strange language. And then there was the body language in itself: it was difficult to know if the Adélies were happy, sad or indifferent. Any interaction between the two species was difficult to quantify: one could not know if they had complimented or insulted the other. And furthermore, the Adélie seemed much more active and with little in terms of self-discipline and of putting off gratification. In fact, in the main waddleways in the colonies it was not uncommon to see one male Adélie try to copulate with another male Adélie. Really! This was all quite barbarous for the Emperors, for both Penguanitarians and Greenies alike. But the Old King, convoking an emergency meeting, would try to quell any of those fears or repulsions.

#

The late-afternoon meeting was a difficult one to conduct. The thousands of Emperors who attended could not hear themselves think with the constant and collective squawking of the

Adélies, who could not keep still, who kept hopping up and down. But for all that, the Old King spoke, his voice as loud as could be. And then members of The Council interrupted the Old King and suggested to him that perhaps it would be best for all concerned if the Adélies were led back to their temporary igloos and then the meeting could be resumed. The Old King nodded, telling the Adélies in their own language that they would be excused since they were obviously suffering from exhaustion and hysterical on account of it.

Once the Adélies were all gone from the meeting, the Old King got into his verbal rhythm. He explained first and foremost that the Adélies would be staying with them for one more night since it was already late and would soon be dark. And the poor mites couldn't be expected to traverse the ice and snow in the dark now, could they? No, better they wait one more night and return to the coast on the morrow.

And then the Old King spoke about the few success stories he had had from the hatchery and got some of the new parents to come up to him and to show off their new chicks to the audience. And although the other penguins clapped their flippers each time a new chick was exhibited, many of them knew that there were far less chicks being hatched now than had been hatching before his taking over the hatchery.

And then the Old King waddled a bit away and the members of The Council took his place. And the members spoke about solidarity and Penguanity and how even though their new visitors, the Adélie penguins, would only be staying with them for another few hours, it behoved all penguins to show the newcomers what colony hospitality could offer them and how they were all going to pull out all the stops for the visitors. It was stated that if the Adélies left tomorrow with good memories from their time in this colony, then they themselves might even try to emulate the Emperors. They themselves might erect igloos and light fires and set nets beneath the ice instead of swimming in the perilous seas. And by emulating the Emperors, the Adélies would become more penguane too. And they would pass on their newfound knowledge of Penguanitarianism to other Adélie colonies and thence on to other colonies from completely different species. Oh yes, the great thing about Nurture and Penguanity was that one good deed would increase tenfold. And what was increased tenfold would go on and in turn increase tenfold. And so on it would go until the world was a better place to inhabit. And as the world would get better, all penguins, wherever they be, could reign in utopia.

Interestingly though, while all these florid speeches were going on, the Adélies instead of going back to their quarters had gone elsewhere. And in there they were having a jolly old time of it. And never had they seen such a quantity of food in their lives in the one place, though the stockpiles were small and too small to feed all the Emperors themselves. But for the Adélies, however, their bodies being tiny when compared to those of Emperors, the stockpiles were massive. And what else was there for the Adélies to do than tuck right into it and gorge themselves silly. And that is precisely what they did. Apart from a pile of squid, which they quickly turned their backs on, they ate everything in the joint, all the krill and every scrap of fish.

#

There was much tension in the colony the next day when it was discovered what had happened. And many half-starved Emperors took it as a penguanal insult that they themselves could barely afford a single fishtail and here were these two-thousand invaders gulping down all sorts of food, and the best sort too. It was a crying shame. And questions would have to be answered.

But the only answer that was given by The Council to the residents of the colony, and it was an answer to a question that had not been asked, was that the Adélies, obviously suffering from the trauma of war and famine, were not acting in their rightful minds. And it just wasn't penguane of these Emperors to be complaining and being so Adéliephobic.

Adéliephobic? the Emperors squawked.

But the members of The Council would not oblige them with a definition of this new coinage, instead just repeating it several times and using it to shoot down any penguin thereafter who said anything that could be construed as insulting to the poor Adélies. Besides, The Council explained, it would not be penguane to send the Adélies off to fend for themselves straight away. No, first they would have to deal with the trauma and strengthen their vigour. Oh yes. And then, only then could they finally depart from the colony.

And when the members of The Council were asked how long that process would take, they responded by saying that with such things, especially the emotional baggage etc., it was very difficult to give it a time frame. It could be days. And if not days, then perhaps just a few weeks to get them back on their feet and prepare them for coastal life once again, and hopefully then, the Adélies, having learnt all there was to learn from the Emperors and The Chosen Penguins, would be able to build a thriving colony with all the creature comforts just like this one had.

CHAPTER 32: FURTHER CULTURAL ENRICHMENT & SPEAR CONTROL

And days passed. And weeks passed. And then a month passed. And it was looking less likely than ever that the Adélies would be upping and leaving. In fact, all of them were moved into sumptuous igloos for free, without having to pay a single gold piece in rent. And furthermore, they were given free coupons by way of stones. And with these stones they could waddle into the Food Wareigloo, point out what they wanted and waddle back out with their flippers full of the best and most nutritious food. It was a travesty, this preferential treatment, many of the Emperors were starting to say. But the aggrieved Emperors would only say this to penguins that they trusted lest a mob of young penguins overhear them and destroy their livelihoods and reputations by squawking the word *Adéliephobia* at them. But yes, in private huddles the Emperors were forthcoming in their disgruntlements, saying things like *We've become second-, no, third-class penguins in our own colony; Our forefathers built this colony and now we're giving it away to strangers; The Adélies have never built anything in their species' whole existence and now they take over our igloos; Why does The Council speak so much about equality and Nurture when the food is not equally shared amongst all?*

And if all that were not bad enough for the common Emperors, The Council declared by decree that for the foreseeable future, and even though it had originally been planned that the Adélies would do so, but, given their emotional trauma and emotional state, no Adélie would have to work. No matter how healthy and energetic he appeared to be. Not one.

And to wreak even more shock upon the angry Emperors, The Council announced a new law, a law that was meant to protect every penguin, whether Emperor, Adélie or Chosen Penguin, and that was Spear Control. From now on, it was declared, only a flipperful of penguins, penguins who would be keeping the peace, would be allowed to carry spears. All other penguins would have to flipper over their spears to The Council.   On hearing this, most Emperors did not bat a membrane, saying to each other that they were willing to give up anything once it meant more protection for all penguins. And some of them said too that The Council knew what it was doing and always knew what it was doing and if this was how penguins in the colony would be safer, then there was no other way of doing it, no other way at all because The Council was smart and would have thought in a hundred different ways and selected the best one, which, as it happened, was this of confiscating all spears.

Other Emperors, however, a few rare others who were the most embittered against the regime, buried their spears under their igloos or in ice crevices a mile outside the colony. They would utter such old refrains as thus:

A penguin who gives up his right to defend himself is a swimmer without flippers.

CHAPTER 33: CRIMINALITY & PC POLICEPENGUINS

Now general crime, apart, that is, from white-collar crime, had been almost non-existent since the colony's inception. The biggest crimes hitherto had been the very occasional murder and that of females kidnapping the chicks of others – and as there were now less chicks in the colony, this latter crime had spiked up of late, spiked up despite the teachings to all females coming of age that fertilized eggs and hatchlings were symbols of their own oppression.

But now crimes were being reported that had never ever happened before. Female Emperors, although much larger than the Adélie males, were not safe from being mugged and raped anywhere since the Adélie males waddled about in gangs of a score or more. Not even Emperor chicks were safe from being raped. And then in the space of five days there had been nine crimes reported of female Emperors being murdered in their igloos at night and their weekly gold pieces for food being taken as well. And, furthermore, there had even been cases of murders where the Adélie male assailant was caught at the scene of the crime copulating with the carcass of the female he had slain.

The law-abiding Emperors, on hearing stories like these, not knowing how to react, went straight to the members of The Council. And the members of The Council explained that such barbarity would not be tolerated, no, by no means would it be tolerated; *rest assured that the full weight of the law will come crushing down on any criminal's head.*

But this seemed to be nothing more than beak service because as time passed more and more of these horrendous crimes were being perpetrated in every part of the colony. And it was said that one Adélie murderer for example who had killed three females in one night by slitting their throats with a dagger he had stolen, had been arrested and thrown into the cage. But not five days had passed when he was seen again at the Food Wareigloo skipping the queue for food with his stone tokens. Well, if the Emperor penguins there didn't half go mental. They set upon the murderer and pecked him to death in no time. And then it was they who were thrown into the cage for murder. And they wouldn't be in there for only five days as he had. In fact, it was said that they would probably end up rotting in the cage for murdering the murderer.

And it was around that time the Old King and The Council called a meeting in which they railed against vigilantism, saying that it was a throwback to barbarity, that an Emperor should not take the law into his own flippers. *And of course the Adélie who was killed was no saint himself, but he deserved to be served by the law and not by barbarity: for Nurture must never in this colony be usurped by barbarity or, better said, Barbarian-reversion.*

And it was around this time that The Council under the advice of the Old King set up the colony's first ever police force. To distinguish themselves from the rest of the civilians when they were on duty, these policepenguins wore a single red feather from some wild bird in the plumes on the back of their head. And very quickly, the other Emperors began to both fear and respect these policepenguins. That single red feather meant that the other penguins would move out of the way of them if they were on the beat. Or if the policepenguins waddled into the Food Wareigloo, they wouldn't have to queue up like the others. No, they could just saunter right up to the counter and, like the Adélie penguins, just point out what they wanted. And with all these perks, it seemed that the most ambitious and corrupt penguins became policepenguins.

And although it was stated in a meeting that the policepenguins were there to serve the public and to arrest those who were committing serious crimes, it soon became apparent that they were turning a blind eye to serious crime and concentrating more on those Emperors who were reported to have criticised the system or the idea of sharing their colony with foreigners, namely King and Adélie penguins, or disclosing corruption from The Council or The Chosen Penguin himself.

Yes, in time the policepenguins became feared by all except the Adélie penguins, who never seemed to alter their terrible behaviour whether they saw a red feather approaching them or not.

CHAPTER 34: PORN, PORN, &, WELL, MORE PORN

Now there had always been a kind of primitive porn and prostitution trade in the colony. It was not spoken about since it was very much frowned upon and taboo, and this was because anything that seemed to side-track young penguins from bonding and reproducing could only be considered wholly unnatural. And what was unnatural could only be bad. What was bad for the colony though it be good for one strange individual was still deemed bad overall. And despite that, all knew that the shady old trade went on. And most important for the majority of the Emperors, it went on far outside the colony. And if it did go on in the colony, it went on behind closed doors.

There was a penguin who had a knack for drawing penguins in the snow, penguins in sexual positions. And when he would be holding his secret exhibition, he would share these drawings with others for a fish or even just a squid tentacle. When gold came into the colony he started accepting that instead. One gold piece to look at one of his drawings for five minutes. And three pieces to look at one of his big drawings for ten minutes. But this little trade of his came to an end when the Old King had got wind of it.

#

The Old King, realizing the wealth that could be generated from tapping into the raging hormones of young penguins and also realizing the usefulness of porn for keeping the mind from concentrating on much else since it was an addictive hobby, went and visited the only ice sculptor in the colony.

Now this ice sculptor had formerly sculpted simple little things such as different shapes and rudimentary sculptures of seals and penguins and whales. And when barter was in use, he would, like the pornographer who drew his pictures in the snow, gain food by these sculptures. But when the Old King visited him, he proposed that henceforth the sculptor work for him, exclusively for him, and sculpt more complicated things, but all involving penguins getting it on.

Taken aback by the proposal, the sculptor had asked the Old King if he was pulling his webbed foot. And the Old King had given him then and there a large gold piece and told him that this was his advanced royalties and there would be a lot more than that if he was willing to sculpt for him from dawn till dusk.

And so, the sculptor began working for the Old King, and the Old King sold the sculptors to customers who came into his jewellers' and gave the secret nod and the secret wink. And then the Old King would lead the customer to the back of his store and let him choose whichever of the many sculptures most turned him on. And these sculptures became a roaring trade for the Old King. At one stage he was making almost more money on these than he was by selling gold jewellery. And often he laughed when he thought of this because at the end of the day he was selling them ice. Just plain ordinary ice that had been shaped by the flippers of the sculptor into a perceived value and lust. And boy was there a fortune to be made in lust!

With the Adélie penguins, themselves very sexualized creatures, the sex trade was there to be exploited to the hilt. And the Old King, aware of this, got the ice sculptor to take on an apprentice and thereby to double production. In past seasons, when the colony had been completely out of food, the Old King had started up a little brothel not far from his complex. Almost all the females in the colony had come there back then and performed all manner of the most grotesque acts on his clients, who had been mostly members of The Council and rich businesspenguins. And in the wee hours the females would waddle back to the colony exhausted and sore all over with a fish in their beaks. To be sure, now with almost two thousand Adélies about, albeit several having been killed already by vengeful Emperors, there was huge scope for the sex industry.

CHAPTER 35: FAILED CONVERSIONS & RELIGIOUS PERSECUTION

The Greenie clerics, although at first keeping a good distance from the newcomers to their colony, could not help but think of how all those new individuals could be brought into their Order and thereby increase the Greenies' clout and influence in the decision-making process of the colony.

At first in ceremonies, the clerics only teased the idea of increasing the flock by bringing in Adélies and letting them admire the night sky and His green curtain of light. And on seeing His beauty, the Adélies would be instantly and miraculously transformed and transfixed, becoming model citizens and adherents to not Moonbird but to Him, as the Greenies themselves were. Yes, He would anoint them here in their very own Greenie Monument by revealing His wonders to them, and thereafter they would forsake Moonbird and become Greenies. And there would be no distinguishable difference thereafter between an Emperor and an Adélie since both were believers and loyal servants of The One True Greenmaker.

#

The Greenies invited hundreds and hundreds of Adélies to a special ceremony one night at the Greenie Monument. A great display in the sky was expected from The Greenmaker, and the clerics were sure that given such a generous display by Him that the Adélies would very quickly become eager to be anointed with His beauty. And failing that, and forgetting that it was the one thing they had not gobbled up in the Food Wareigloo that time when they had routed it, the Greenie clergy had bought two full tonnes of squid: for if they could not fill their spirits with The Greenmaker's love, at least they could fill their stomachs and convert them all thereby.

But alas, though Greenies stood side by side with the Adélies, it could be noticed that while some were looking at His green curtain of light and following its progress with their craned necks across the sky, the majority of the Adélies were staring statically at the moon. Try as they might to point the Adélies in the direction of His green curtain of light, the Adélies' gaze would quickly return to that of the moon. Though the ceremony had been held with the highest expectations and excitement, even the most optimistic Greenie clerics had to admit that thus far the event had been an abysmal failure. There would be no converting the Adélies by way of the spirit. No matter how hard they tried and no matter how elegantly His green curtain of light played across the sky from horizon to horizon, they would never forsake their Moonbird.

And therefore, Plan B was begun. The clerics and some of the laypenguins corralled the Adélies over to the tables, which were covered. Lifting off the covers, they presented their guests with the two tonnes of squid. The finest squid that could be bought in the Food Wareigloo. In fact, the clerics had to call in all sorts of special favours and pull many a string to acquire this sumptuous feast, not to mention the great expense of gold it had cost the Order's coffers.

But their guests threw their faces away from the food. Many of them retched by the mere sight of the squid. One of the senior Adélies squawked and flapped his flippers wildly. And then there was a stampede of Adélies out of the Greenie Monument. Perplexed, the Greenies, both clerics and laypenguins, scratched their heads and beaks. Just what had happened? Why would all the Adélies turn their beaks up at such tasty fare? And not only that, but seem offended by being offered it? Well, they didn't know in that moment, but they would find out the next day courtesy of one of the Old King's sons translating it for them: for the Adélies the squid with its black ink was a dirty animal. And it was part of their culture and belief system that no matter how hungry an Adélie would be, he was never to eat even a morsel of squid. Should he do so, Moonbird would let Himself fall from the sky and onto the sinner, thereby crushing him.

#

And if things weren't bad enough for the Greenies, they were going to get a whole lot worse. The most zealous of the Adélies took the Greenies' Order as an absolute affront to their own. How could penguins, they thought whilst shaking their heads, be so besotted by something moving in the sky and disappearing when Moonbird was there in a perfect circle and relatively still, His progress slow and not so fleeting? No, these Greenies, the Adélie zealots summed up, were infidels. And infidels could not be entertained whatsoever. Infidels would be given three choices in their coastal lands: convert, die or pay a hefty tax by way of food. Yes indeed, those were the only options ever open to an infidel.

But of course that night in the Greenie Monument, though much offended by the constant prodding and pointing out of the green light in the sky by the Emperor clerics, these Adélie clerics had brayed as though amazed even though deep inside them much resentment was boiling up to the surface. No, the Greenies would be dealt with in time for having offended them and Moonbird, and furthermore, for just having the audacity to believe in deities that were not He, Moonbird, or The Silver One.

#

Attacks on Greenies began in earnest. Several foiled attempts were made on stealing The Sacred Greenstone and destroying it. Greenie females in particular were sought out amongst the other Emperor females to be beaten and raped. And now services at the Greenie Monument were troubled not by egg-throwing females of empowerment but Adélies, who pecked at both male, female and chick Emperor penguins that were filing in. Something, the Greenies said, would have to be done about the Adélies. Something would have to be done. They could not go on like this. Their wick was burning down.

And to all of this, the clerics tried to calm them down, to de-beak them by saying that every time one of them was attacked by an Adélie, that instead of attacking him back, they should simply extend The Flipper of Greenliness. Yes, that would be what He up there would expect of them since He was vehemently against violence, unless of course He Himself was feeling wrathful for something the Greenies had done or not done. But for the most part, and down here on the ice, He was vehemently against violence, against all forms of violence no matter what the species or subspecies. And the best way for the Greenies to stop violence was not through beak-to-beak conflict but rather by simply extending the Flipper of Greenliness to the enemy. Nothing defused tension and anger more than the extension of the Flipper of Greenliness because at the end of the day the main tenet of the Greenie Order was forgiveness. Forgiveness and compassion. There were no real enemies out there. A perceived enemy when all was said and done was just a penguin one hadn't befriended yet. And whether it were a Penguanitarian or an Adélie that pecked you in the face, you as a Greenie, if you really were a Greenie because this was the acid test, well, you would respond with kindness. You would prove yourself a Greenie, a servant of the Father of Forgiveness up there in the night sky with His warm green curtain of light. Yes, you too would respond with kindness by extending the Flipper of Greenliness. And once you had done this, all would be forgiven, and both the Adélies and the Penguanitarians would come around to understanding His love for them though they not be practicing His ways.

#

Well, many left the congregation after the sermon on the Flipper of Greenliness, cursing the cleric and cursing their own order. If an Adélie or Penguanitarian attacked them, they agreed, the last thing they would be extending to them would be the Flipper of Greenliness. If anything, they would be extending them the Flipper of Knockout. Others however bethought this advice by the cleric to be wholesome and wise, and when they were attacked by gangs of Adélies who squawked at them for being infidels, they would confidently extend the Flipper of Greenliness. Suffice it to say that quite a number of Greenies waddled about with broken flippers. And unfortunately for them, the bodybird still in the cage, there was nobody around to set the bones right. And as things worsened, services in the Greenie Monument had to be postponed because on one night some penguins, nobody knew who, but it was presumed they were Adélies since their faeces was different than that of Emperors, well, yeah, some penguins had defecated all over the ice floor of the Greenie Monument and the great place had to be vacated for some time in order to be cleansed.

CHAPTER 36: A FAMILIAR STRANGER CALLS

He came to them in a blizzard. And although there was something familiar about him, nobody could really admit to themselves that they had ever met him before. He was a tall old Emperor penguin with a black patch over one eye and he brayed in an accent that was slightly exotic. He called himself One-Eye, and so all called him by that name. Little did they know that he was an infiltrator. And little did they know that he had been one of the Elders of Instinct, those who had been expelled from the colony long ago. In fact, he had been the one who had had his eye pecked out by the Penguanitarians.

    His real mission, obviously enough, he would not make known to them. His fake mission without a moment's hesitation he disclosed: he was come to find out about Penguanitarianism. He had heard word of it from afar and was much interested in knowing more. Likewise were many of his brothers and sisters in his colony interested in knowing more about it. Such great and amazing things had he heard about this colony here. And so great was the hunger for knowledge in his colony that the main leaders thereof had sent him here to gather information and to emulate all that was good in this place when he would return whence he had come.

    Well, if this visitor, this penguin called One-Eye, did not half get the royal treatment from all the top brass! Hearing of his intentions, they were all over him like a rash. The twenty-four members of The Council brought him hither and thither to show off this and show off that, to show off all the great social accomplishments. The businesspenguins invited him to a banquet and there explained to him the merits of dealing in gold as opposed to that of barter, and how gold, and gold alone, was responsible for the building boom he saw before him now, igloos as far as his single eye could see.

And the Old King even invited him to his complex and served him the best of food and the cleanest of freshwater, and there gave him insights into how porn could be a great asset to any colony and also how empowering females was the penguane thing to do – in fact, without female empowerment there could be no Penguanitarianism. Yes, once female empowerment was on the wax then all sorts of great things could be brought into a colony to enrich it further, including for example the bringing in of other penguin species. No, there was nothing nicer and more penguane than living in the melting pot and seeing different types of faces and different-sized bodied and different plumes in all their hues and listening to different squawks. Nothing better. To be sure, the Old King, explained, when he himself had arrived here from Tierra del Fuego where all his subspecies had more or less been slain, a genocide having been committed against them, this colony here had been a rather dull place. Of course, nobody would think that now, but it had been very glum and dreary indeed. The same old faces. The one old language. And there had even been these superstitious old penguins called Elders of Tomfoolery who believed in some silly notion called instinct or whatnot. Well, fortunately, the Penguanitarians here being penguane creatures did the only penguane thing they could do and expelled those meddlesome old farts from this wonderful colony.

On hearing all this, especially the latter part, One-Eye felt like grabbing the Old King there and then and squeezing the living daylights out of him. But he quickly suppressed that sensation and instead nodded politely. There would be time for all of that. Nothing could be done until the time was right. He was not here as an assassin but as a spy. As calmly as he could muster, he asked the Old King about justice and punishment and how such notions were treated here in the colony. What sort of criminals did they have and what sorts of crimes were being carried out?

Well, the Old King reeled off crime after crime. He related to One-Eye the murders that had been perpetrated by Emperor penguins who had no doubt a case of Barbarian-reversion and Adéliephobia. They had attacked a few hapless Adélies and stricken them dead. And he spoke of a right brigand who was known as the bodybird and how he was caught plotting and scheming and trying to bring the whole colony into anarchy – another case, no doubt, of Barbarian-reversion. Yes, the Old King explained to One-Eye, there was nothing worse than Barbarian-reversion and wherever it reared its ugly head it had to be annihilated. Barbarian-reversion was a virus, a sickness that could destroy everything they had worked so hard to build and nurture. He himself due to an increase in Barbarian-reversion could no longer waddle around the colony alone, now being escorted by a dozen securitypenguins all the time. And why? Not because of anything he'd done of course. If anything, he, the Old King, had done more for this place than anyone else. To be sure, if it hadn't been for his marvellous and ice-breaking innovations, they'd all be out there living in the Dark Ages. And for all that, would you believe it? Could you countenance it? But for all that there were penguins out there, Emperor penguins who wanted to kill him, The Chosen Penguin, Doctor Penguanity? And he couldn't count, just couldn't count though he was good at counting, how many times a death threat had been made against him in this place. Oh yes, his life was in constant peril. As were the lives of his sons and daughters and grandchicks. The word *ingrates* could be used to describe such penguins who wanted to do away with the Old King and his family after all the sacrifices he had made for them. *Traitors* too could describe these penguins. Or *turnfeathers*. But Barbarian-reversion was what it was when one looked at it from an objective point of view. Barbarian-reversion and a strong case of Anti-Aptenodytecism thrown in for good measure. Oh yes, Anti-Aptenodytecism. A pathology that was even worse than Barbarian-reversion. You could say it was Barbarian-reversion on steroids. For some reason or other, and try as he might, the Old King just couldn't understand why, but for some reason or other penguins who were not King penguins were hatched with a hatred for King penguins. An intrinsic hatred. Some Kings even said that the hatred for them by other penguin species was there even before the egg itself was laid. A sort of hatred that was passed down through the generations to all penguins to hate The Chosen Penguins. And why oh why would all penguin species secretly or publicly hate The Chosen Penguins?! Maybe it was down to jealousy. Good old-fashioned jealousy and begrudgery. Maybe it was down to them all being possessed with an Anti-Aptenodytic demon that hated for hatred's sake The Chosen Penguin. Either way, there was no cure for the condition. And the only way for the King penguin to survive was to rule with an iron flipper over them all. That was the only way. Of course, that often led to rebellion. But rebellion was only collateral damage. What mattered was that The Chosen Penguin ruled the roost because it was he and he alone who could bring forth utopia here on ice. Yes, only he could stop one penguin species from massacring another. Only he could bring penguins the world over to a state of civilization and harmony.

On hearing all this squawking on Anti-Aptenodytecism, One-Eye almost brayed out in laughter. But he suppressed it. And he then tried to suppress his shuddering body that was shuddering due to the inward laughter. Did not the Old King know that both King and Emperor penguins were both from that same genus? To say that Emperor penguins were being Anti-Aptenodytic would mean literally that they hated themselves, were full of self-loathing. For a second he thought of stating this error of speech or of semantics to the Old King but remembered that he must not cast suspicion on himself. No, it was better to play the part of the hick from out of town who was here to seek Penguanitarianism and its Progress and Nurture. And so, it would be wise to let the Old King prattle on.

And prattle on he surely did. The poor, poor Adélie penguins, he explained, had had to endure no end of pain and suffering from these Barbarian-reverters, these uncouth Emperors. Adéliephobia was a sign of a penguin who was on the road to Barbarian-reversion and if the right penalties or incarceration methods were not used, the penguin in question could worsen. And then there would be no going back for the individual. Either he or she would have to be locked up in the cage for life or executed. A cull though, the Old King lamented, was still not on the agenda since the Penguanitarians believed it was inpenguane. But if the Old King had his way, then by golly there would be a great old culling every day of the week for those who were picking on the poor Adélies, the little penguins who had suffered so much and who were still going through trauma, trauma they had picked up from their war-torn colonies. And for all the complaints levelled against the Adélies, it was they who had brought his sons and their wives and chicks back safely to the Old King. The Adélie, instead of being considered a primitive penguin, was much more suave and sophisticated and generous than any Emperor penguin alive. One-Eye pinched himself hard so as not to laugh at this last statement.

And as much as the Old King explained every facet of the colony, rightly or wrongly, it quickly became apparent to One-Eye that the Old King wanted to know more about his colony. First and foremost, the Old King asked him where it was. To this, One-Eye gave him the wrong directions and the wrong waddling distance too.

And once it had been disclosed that in One-Eye's colony they had already built igloos and discovered fire and fashioned both nets and spears, the Old King thought that perhaps he himself would not be leaving Antarctica so soon after all: for when things would become bloody here, and there was no doubting that, he and his kin could skedaddle off to another colony that was ripe for the taking and there begin anew. And getting suddenly giddy with excitement, the Old King came out with a flurry of questions: how many penguins lived there; the demographics broken down into male, female, chick and eggs; were there any spiritual Orders like the Greenies; if unfertilized eggs were a common occurrence in One-Eye's colony; if gender equality had even begun to be a thing there; could the females choose whether to have their eggs fertilized or not; could they also choose whether the hatchling had the right to hatch or not. Of this last question, One-Eye trembled with anger – never had he heard of such an unnatural scenario and he wondered if that was precisely what was going on here; and never had he felt as outraged as he felt in this moment!

And the Old King was studying him now and seemed to be aware of this outrage. And so One-Eye had to check himself once again and change the subject. He let the Old King know that he would be staying here for five days and in those five days he expected to learn much, both from him, such a kind host, and the rest of the penguins, be they Emperors or Adélies or The Chosen Penguins. The Old King was must delighted when he heard his guest name him and his subspecies as The Chosen Penguins and then he became very friendly and bubbly, the guarded appearance on his face suddenly dropping. He told One-Eye that he believed it was destiny that he had come to this colony. And it was due to this destiny that they were here now having this ever so interesting beak-a-beak. Yes, it must have been, just must have been, written in the stars.

And so, One-Eye could stay the night here at his complex and whatever he wanted he had only to say the word. If he wanted fish, then he only had to ask for it. If he wanted more freshwater, then it was done. And if he wanted a sleeping partner for the night, whether male or female, and if male whether Emperor or Adélie, or if chicks were his thing, then that too could be arranged. What mattered, said the Old King, was that he was comfortable here and felt right at home. *My igloo is your igloo*, said the Old King holding out his flipper. And performing the custom, though with much reluctance, One-Eye held the little flipper of the Old King.

And before the conversation ended for the night, the Old King explained how their two colonies could be brought into the same orbit through trade in gold, through Penguanitarianism, through equality regardless of gender or species, and through peace. Yes, peace. Peace was essential. Peace was the difference between Nurture and barbarity.

So, on the morrow, One-Eye would be free to waddle all around the colony. And no door would be closed to him. And all the workings of the colony would be explained to him at length and shown to him. And in five days' time when he would be due to leave and return to his colony, the Old King promised to send a delegation of his best and brightest with him to help with the cultural and progressive transition that would surely take place there. Because One-Eye's colony, the Old King warned, his face suddenly very serious, although it had made great strides by the sound of it, would not last if it did not embrace Modernity. Yes, Modernity was the future. And the past was deep in the shadow of barbarity. And so, what mattered was constantly changing things, constantly improving things.

If it's not broke, laughed the Old King as he departed to his own quarters, *break it and fix it; fix it the penguane way.*

#

One-Eye left the Old King's complex early the next morning and made his way to the colony. He noticed that throughout his journey thither, even though he veered off the main waddleway several times, that six henchpenguins were following him. And every time One-Eye turned around to look at them, the henchpenguins stopped waddling and pretended to preen each other.

#

Here in the daylight and now blizzard-free, One-Eye was able to see the depravity and the indigence that lay all around him in this, his old colony. Adélies were defecating here and there without regard to whoever was watching them. They were also squabbling amongst themselves and accosting Emperor females and chicks. And how weak and sickly those Emperor penguins looked. They had become sticklike and many could barely waddle a few yards without having to stop and catch their breath. Great igloos that One-Eye had helped in constructing were now partitioned into a number of tiny compartments wherein labourers slept for few hours, the rest of their long day being taken up by the working day or night. It seemed, apart from the district in which the members of The Council and the rich businesspenguins lived, that the idea of an igloo for one family or for one new breeding pair was now a thing of the past.

#

And the Food Wareigloo had gone to wrack and ruin as well. The orderly lines of yesteryear were now bedlam, penguins jostling for space, trying to get a few more inches up towards where the food was flippered out. And here it seemed that the pecking order was that of rich Emperors, then Adélies and finally the common Emperor penguins, the latter lacking the vim to jostle, only able to wait for the rest of them to clear and then go and get the scraps. It was embarrassing and soul-shattering for One-Eye to witness this, to witness his kinfolk being left to squabble weakly over scraps. And as much as the sight of all those Adélies squawking and flapping their flippers irritated him to no end, it was more the sight of his own species that made him seethe with rage: the sell-outs, the traitors, the penguins who had feathered their nests too much and to the detriment of the whole colony.

#

If the Food Wareigloo rankled him, the hatchery certainly was not going to offer him any sort of antidote. He was informed there by one of the Old King's daughters that most of the eggs in front of him were unfertilized.

Now, unfertilized eggs in One-Eye's day had been almost unheard of. As has already been stated, in olden times unfertilized eggs were considered a complete anomaly. And here he was not looking at one of them but dozens and dozens.

The five eggs marked with a red splotch were those that

were fertilized but that would soon be destroyed. Now how One-Eye restrained himself from losing it altogether was beyond his ken. But restrain himself once again he did. And though overcome with the paternal instinct that was stronger in his species than in any other and though he had thought of taking one or two of those fertilized eggs and hiding them under the flab of skin above his feet, he had to think of the bigger plan. No point in getting caught and thereby scuppering the entire mission, a mission that not only he had a flipper in but which all the penguins who were back there in the other colony had carefully planned too. No, there would have to be sacrifices.

And even though it was hard not to rescue those fertilized eggs that were in reach, the only positive thing he could think of was that this madness here, this nightmare, would soon end. And as the Old King's daughter led him into another compartment of the hatchery and he nodded politely, he clung to the old saying that went thus:

It is always darkest before the dawn.

\#

On the fourth day, although he had many pressing engagements with all the high-flyers of the colony, One-Eye, shadowed at a short distance by those same henchpenguins, visited the place that was more on his list than any other. One-Eye went to the guardigloo with all its cages.

The warden there explained to One-Eye that he had not been informed by any of the members of The Council or by The Chosen Penguin of any visitor coming to check the place out. And so, One-Eye, knowing this warden and almost forgetting to speak in his pretend foreign accent, squawked at him in a brutal manner and told him that if he did not open up all access to him this very instance, then he himself would have to leave and return with The Chosen Penguin, at whose complex he was currently residing, or did the warden not know this? On hearing such a rebuke and such a threat, the warden's resilience buckled and he waddled to it and opened up the main door that led into the corridor, where on both sides were to be found many cages, and in each cage stood or lay a penguin, most of whom were Emperors. And the air made bitter and toxic by guano was suddenly nauseating.

As One-Eye waddled down the corridor, he could hear the hissing coming from some of the cages, and each time he looked to see where the hissing was coming from his eyes were met by those of an Adélie penguin. They were squawking up quite a rumpus as he passed by them, those Adélies, but One-Eye could not understand a whit of their language. And their cages seemed to have a pinkish glow about them that was due to their mounds of guano. No penguin seemed to poop as much as the Adélie. Did the guards here not get the prisoners to clean out their cages daily as they had back in the day even though there had hardly been any prisoners in those days? Surely the fumes in here would not be healthy. They could drive a penguin mad. And perhaps all of them in here were mad now, at least madder than they had been before they'd been incarcerated. He saw one Adélie pecking at a wound on his breast and then drinking the blood that came spurting out therefrom.

Down at the very end of the corridor and to the left did he find whom he had been seeking. The bodybird was standing, staring at the wall, seemingly oblivious to both sound and movement. And when One-Eye addressed him in his normal voice, the bodybird slowly turned around and waddled forward. He looked through the vertical trunks of driftwood that acted as bars at One-Eye, and looked at him as though he were looking at a ghost. His mind went through a series of questions as he stated at One-Eye:

Could it be him? Could it really be him? Is he alive or is he dead or is he a figment of my imagination? Or is it I who is dead? Is it I who is the ghost?

One-Eye was able to fit his right flipper in between the bars and give the bodybird a good slap on the beak to take him out of his reverie. And then the bodybird became relaxed and was like the bodybird of old. And like that bodybird of old, he watched and listened and did not interrupt.

One-Eye explained to him that this would only be a flying visit. He would have liked to get into conversation about the degeneracy and unnaturalness that was now permeating all aspects of this colony, but there was no time for that. There was only time to let the bodybird know that a week from now there would be a great reckoning. A week from now things were going to change around here, and change for the good. All depended on the weather. And all depended on faith in the Emperor species to overcome the parasite that had been upon them over and over again since the beginning. And if all went well this time, they would crush the parasite for once and for all. And if they could not rid the world of the parasite, then at least they could rid Antarctica of it for many, many millennia to come.

And so, the bodybird was told to be ready. The bodybird was told to spread the word in the corridor, but only to those whom he trusted with his very life. He and they were all to be ready for the day of reckoning. And there would be no perching on the fence. You were either going to fight for the Emperor penguin species or you were going to be annihilated. And when they would come to break the Emperor prisoners out of their cages a week from now, they would all be provisioned with spears and weapons better than spears. And they would be expected to fight for their lives. Their liberty was only guaranteed if they were willing to fight for their lives and that of the species.

The bodybird put his right flipper through the bars of his cage. One-Eye took it in his flipper and squeezed it. No more was said. No more needed to be said. One-Eye turned and waddled back down the corridor amongst a cacophony of hisses and incomprehensible squawks. He went out through the exit and away from the nauseating and eye-watering air.

#

On the morning before his departure from the colony, there was much fanfare amongst the VIPs (Very Important Penguins). The Old King was there. As were his sons and daughters and grandchicks. As were all the businesspenguins. As were the other members of The Council. It had been agreed that the delegation that would accompany One-Eye back to his colony would be comprised of one of the Old King's sons, one of his daughters, two male members of The Council and two businesspenguins, these latter being the biggest and richest building contractors. This delegation, which would spend three days in that other colony, would consult the Emperors in that colony on such matters as trade in gold, the property and rental market, the tenets of Penguanitarianism, gender equality and female liberation, and of course the privatization of such things as hatcheries and food depots. For the VIPs there really was a great sense of being on the cusp of something great, of bringing Progress to a new society, of cornering a new market. All of the VIPs were constantly braying with joy and flapping each other on the back.

The only ones who were a bit disappointed there and felt as though they had been left out in the cold were the Greenie clerics. They had pleaded and grovelled to no end so as to be able to send one penguin from their Order to spread the love of The Greenmaker in this new colony but had been denied; however, notwithstanding this outright rejection, they clung to the hope that as this colony and the new one would eventually merge into a union they could strengthen over there what was weakening here, and thereby maintain some semblance of power and authority.

Off they went. One-Eye led the way, the wrong way, since he had to go in the direction that he had given to the Old King that first night in his complex. The delegation waddled after him, now and then turning back to the crowds that saw them off and waving a flipper to them. There was much braying and squawking and flapping until One-Eye and the delegation disappeared over the horizon. Of the six penguins that made up the delegation that had left, only two would make it back. And instead of making it back in the agreed three days, they would not return until a whole week later. And One-Eye would return with them.

One-Eye and two-hundred other Emperors

CHAPTER 37: NO-SHOW & CONTINGENCY PLANS

The Old King was satisfied at how things were panning out, notwithstanding what he deemed to be a serious increase in the colony of Anti-Aptenodytecism. He was, however, content in knowing that perhaps not *if* but *when* this colony here would go belly-up there would be another close at flipper to exploit or, as he put it, *to enrich*. He waddled off to check on his contingency plans and to re-check those plans.

In the last number of days, he and his sons and daughters had been making various nightly excursions to the shingle beach and the glacier. And with them they had transported half of the Old King's gold and the silver piece with which he had entered the colony that first time. And they transported plenty of food from his stockpile too. Plenty of food and freshwater. They calculated that the glacier would be breaking off and forming an iceberg soon, very soon. And timing would be everything.

A King penguin did not need to be told by others whether his neck was on the chopping block or not. He just knew. And he knew when that time was nigh. And the Old King and his progeny without discussing it amongst themselves knew that this colony which had served them so well and for so long was about to fall. And with its falling would come an unprecedented amount of Anti-Aptenodytecism. And with Anti-Aptenodytecism abounding, a King penguin had to rail in his feathers and get very busy indeed. With Anti-Aptenodytecism abounding, the King penguin either struck out for icefields new or would meet a most gruesome end. So it had been in the beginning. And so it was now. And somehow that knowledge had come down through the ages and embedded itself in the King penguins' genes. Nothing was written down. There was no writing. Nothing was passed down orally either to the King penguin. Everything was just known. And what was known could only be deemed just or unjust from the perspective of the one species. But if one species, however, could convince others of what was just or unjust, then that species could do really well in the eternal struggle, could really prosper at the other species' expense. If the Old King had ever thought about it to himself, he might have summed it up thus: what is hatched to be exploited must surely be exploited, and what is hatched to exploit must surely exploit.

But the Old King after having transported half his gold to a site close to the glacier was now caught up in two separate plans. The one involving the glacier/iceberg would be one fraught with dangers and one that could be the end of him and his legacy, though not the species since the King penguin was much more populous that had been admitted to the Emperors. The other plan, on the other flipper, involved waiting to hear back from the delegation who had gone to check out the new colony. If the new colony turned out to be a great virgin society ready to be deflowered, then the King and his progeny could up sticks and move there and let this place go to ruin as it surely would in, if not a matter of days, in a matter of weeks.

The King penguins had the sacrificial trait if their environment called upon such a trait to become activated. If a King penguin were having a hard time of it from other species, the King penguins would come to his or her aid. If the King penguin were, however, having a hard time of it from another King penguin, well, then things would be left well alone. And now, caught in between two exit plans, the Old King decided what best to do in order to safeguard the species. The cohesion of the

King penguin species was ironclad when required.

Ironically enough, although the King penguin could preach the tenets of Penguanitarianism all day and night long, he did so as the self-appointed Chosen Penguin. And from such a lofty vantage point, he could not but somehow loathe those other penguin species such as the Emperor that swallowed such theoretical swill hook, line and sinker. Once again, if the Old King had ever thought about it to himself, he would have summed it up in that same sentence: what is hatched to be exploited must surely be exploited, and what is hatched to exploit must surely exploit.

He would wait for his son and daughter to return from the new colony to relay him with information thereof. And if all sounded above-board, then he would accompany one son and the family of that son, and one daughter and the chick of that daughter, to the new colony. He would leave behind one son and the family of that son, and one daughter and the chick of that daughter in the old colony. And as for the rest, as for the other son and his family, and the other daughter and her chick, they would stay here close to the glacier and ride it across the sea when it had become an iceberg, thereby staking new territories for the species. Yes, the Old King would hedge his bets. Because what mattered was the King species. What mattered was that, come what may, the species would somehow continue, and this continuance was down to a set pattern of behaviours that had served them since the days of the primordial soup and would serve them yet again. What was tried was trusted. And what was tried a billion times was trusted a billion times more.

In the meantime, as the days passed, as food prices shot up further, and as more and more Emperors became iglooless, as Adélie penguins committed countless crimes, as vigilantism became the status quo, the Old King tripled his security team and tripled the salaries of each securitypenguin too. The only thing that seemed to stave off out-and-out rebellion from erupting was the constant excitement intentionally being promulgated among the masses in regard to the new colony and how soon the delegation would be back with tidings of good news, good news for everyone regardless of species or gender or belief system. Oh yes, good news for all.

#

But the good news on the expected day did not come. There was neither blubber nor feather of any of the delegation. No silhouette broke the distant horizon. And then more days passed. And as each day passed so too did the tension in the colony and the sly hisses in the back alleys of what would soon be done, what needed to be done. Because if nothing was done, then they were all doomed. And risking life was better than certain death. And these hisses came from all the different factions. They came from Emperors of no distinction. They came from the Adélies. They came from Penguanitarians. They even came from followers who had tried out much to their shock and maimed appendages the Flipper of Greenliness.

#

On the sixth day after the delegation had left with One-Eye, the Old King and his family made their final preparations, but they were preparations solely in regard to pining all hope on the glacier/iceberg. They began transporting in earnest the rest of the gold early that morning to the shingle beach and thence to the glacier. With rudimentary chisels they were able to make holes in the glacier and therein insert the gold pieces and food and little bags of freshwater. And these holes were then sealed simply by pouring seawater over them, which froze solid in no time at all. It was tough manual work. And how the King penguins loathed manual work! But there was nobody they could hire to carry out this task for them, nobody whom they could trust apart from those of their own blood, their own tribe – otherwise, in no time at all would it be spread like wildfire throughout the colony that the King penguins, The Chosen Penguins, were moving all their wealth to the coast along with food and freshwater. And the Emperor penguins, most of whom were starving, would be there on the coast in no time with flippers out for food and their beaks ready to tear every last King penguin asunder.

    By afternoon, all the King penguin's wealth had been moved and embedded into the glacier, far beyond the assumed fracture line whence it would break off from the mainland and bob off to wherever destiny would decide. And now, they would rest here until the seismic event would take place. They would spend the night on the glacier and listen to it creaking its way to freedom and thereby to their own.

CHAPTER 38: RECONQUISTA COMMENCETH

They came the following day at noon. A score of Emperors. They made one line across the horizon. And with them were the son and daughter of the Old King. And both of them were gagged and bound. And this score of Emperors stopped approaching when they were some two hundred metres off from the colony. They were waiting. And it could be seen that they were armed with daggers and spears.

  The Emperors from the colony that made up the police were rallied within minutes. And they too stood with spears and daggers, gazing at those penguins out there and wondering just exactly what they hoped to achieve when they were so clearly outnumbered. They gazed and waited for orders to come from above. And then The Council arrived, all its members apart from the Old King's daughters, one of whom, as has already been stated, was out there as though bait being used by those trespassers. The Council ordered the opening up of the weaponry depot, and every male was provisioned with a spear and a dagger. Now with five-thousand resident Emperor penguins weaponized, those goons out there, even if they had another thousand goons coming up the rear to support them, The Council guffawed, would be quickly tobogganed through or captured.

  But unfortunately, and the members of The Council had

to reluctantly admit it to themselves, it was not as simple as that. The problem lay with the prisoners the ruffians out there had brought with them. Had they been any other penguins from the colony, The Council would not have thought twice of sending out enough penguins to slaughter these outlaws. But these hostages were no ordinary penguins: they were Chosen Penguin hostages. If anything happened to either of the Old King's offspring, if one feather were harmed on their heads, the members of The Council felt that there would be serious repercussions for them.

And where was The Old King anyway? Should he not be working in his jewellers' now? Or checking in on his daughters in the hatchery? But no King penguins could be found in the colony. How very strange! And so, a messenger was sent off to seek the Old King at his complex. But on arriving there, the securitypenguins told the messenger that the Old King and his progeny had gone off on a little trip, a little trip towards the coast. Perplexed and not knowing what to do now, the messenger waddled back to the colony and informed The Council that the Old King and his family were not at his complex either. And so, The Council sent out a party of twenty policepenguins to meet the trespassers and find out just exactly what their demands were.

The Greenie clerics, sensing that something very bloody and malevolent was about to go down here in the colony, gathered their flock and advised them all to seek sanctuary in the Greenie Monument. Apart from several who were armed with spears and daggers and who felt an obligation to serve The Council and the colony in their hour of need, all Greenies did what the clerics told them to do. There in the Greenie Monument would they hunker down and wait out the storm they predicted was about to arrive.

#

Meanwhile the guardigloo was easily overtobogganed by a flipperful of invading Emperors, among them One-Eye. The guards on duty there were commanded to lay down their spears and to join them in taking over the colony, or as One-Eye himself put it, in retaking the colony, in The Reconquista. Two of the guards obliged without a moment's hesitation. One did not and was quickly slain.

The bodybird was freed first and he picked out from the cages those Emperors who were rebels and who could be trusted to take up spears against The Chosen Penguins and The Council. The rest, including eight Adélies, were bludgeoned in their cages.

Coming up the rear of the colony and unbeknownst to the residents were some two-thousand invading Emperor penguins, a fifth of which were armed with what had hitherto never been seen before. A new weapon. A revolution in warfare. The harpoon. And amidst this force was Plucky, his chest stuck out in defiance to whatever would come his way in this battle. And what first came the way of Plucky and his army was the Food Wareigloo, outside of which were gathered a thousand Adélie penguins. Most of the Adélies were unarmed but some had managed to acquire daggers.

The first line of Emperors made gestures for the Adélies to shoo, to leave the colony post-haste or else. But the Adélies did not seem to understand this and set upon the Emperors. And so the first bloodbath began in earnest. And it lasted a good half an hour in all. Fifty Emperors were killed in the onslaught while all one thousand Adélies were stricken down and would flap their flippers no more.

#

The Council had finally got wind of the invading army and so sent forth four-thousand Emperors and the nine-hundred-and-odd Adélies to liquidate it. The Adélies, however, did not understand what they were to do and so scattered about throughout the colony, going on a sort of rampage of plunder and rape and murder. When the four-thousand resident Emperors came into view of the invading army, the latter fled and the former gave chase.

Little did the resident Emperors know, but this was another ruse by the invaders. After a mile or so the invaders crossed a ravine atop which were long pieces of driftwood that acted as bridges. And once all were over on the far side, these pieces of driftwood were removed. Well, the resident Emperors waddled right up to the edge of the ravine and started sneezing salt. Some started flinging their spears across, several of which found their mark right in the middle of the breasts of the invaders, who fell down and did not get back up.

Once this flurry of spears had ended, Plucky waddled right up to the ravine and addressed those on the other side. He told them who he was even though he was sure that many of them knew who he was already. And he gave them one command: if they were willing to join forces with him and the other Emperors, their lives would be spared; if, however, they chose to continue serving The Council and that cursed King penguin, then this would be their last day on ice. And to demonstrate if they were going to fight with him or against him, Plucky indicated that those who fell into the former category should get down onto their bellies now. And out of the four-thousand resident Emperors, five-hundred immediately got down onto their bellies, many of which were blood relatives of him who had given this option. And these penguins who were now prostrate on the snow were about to be set upon by the rest of their comrades when the harpoons appeared all along the other side and were shot. And almost every single harpoon found its mark, the first line of resident Emperors, some two-thousand of them, falling down, a pool of blood staining their white breasts and seeping out into the snow, turning it pink. And now it dawned on the rest of the resident Emperors that the tables had turned on them; that they were now the minority army given that five-hundred of their members who had been prostrate were now risen and engaging them in close flipper-to-flipper combat. And with that, the lengths of driftwood were placed back over the ravine and the invading force crossed once again and joined the melee.

All in all, five hundred of the invaders' forces, many of

whom had been the resident Emperors who had turned on their comrades by lying prostrate, lost their lives. The invading army kept crossing the ravine and attacking those that were left. This fighting went on for some time. In the end, of the resident army a mere twenty of them survived, all waddling as fast as their little legs could carry them back to the colony. But none was to get there, the harpoons taking them out with surprise, the bodies keeling over and rolling into stillness in the snow that again turned into a pink sludge. There was silence. And then there was a great battlesquawk as Plucky and his comrades got ready to toboggan back into the colony.

#

The Council did not know that the army they had sent to destroy the invading forces had been liquidated. They did not therefore know the current precariousness of their position. They did not know that Emperor-soldier to Emperor-soldier they were now outnumbered almost two to one. The twenty penguins they had sent out to open dialogue with those criminals came back and told them that the said criminals out there were not going to set any demands until the Old King made an appearance. Hearing this infuriated the members of The Council. Were they meant to wait here all day and all night for him while the colony was being laid siege to? But what other choice did they have? If one took the decision to do anything and it turned out to be the wrong decision, then he could lose his place in The Council and would become just an ordinary penguin forever more. And so, they still waited, trying to figure out what to do but knowing that they would end up doing nothing whatsoever.

Then some members of The Council bespoke voting. Voting on whether to send enough Emperors out there to slaughter those twenty criminals with the two hostages. Damn the Old King and damn his brood but invaders must be dealt with at all costs! Besides, we do not negotiate with terrorists! But the other members of The Council overruled them and made a mental note of this treachery, which they penguanally planned to relay to the Old King when he would return to the colony and all would be back to normal. But then they heard the battlesquawk from afar. And the blood froze in their veins on hearing it.

They dillydallied no more. The remaining thousand be-speared and be-daggered Emperors were sent to meet the invaders head-on, but not before having had to listen to a rousing speech from one of the members of The Council, who reminded them that they, and only they, were now what stopped this colony from falling into barbarity; only they were the difference in whether this colony would continue progressing or be waylaid into the cold exposure of the dark times. Their effort if strong enough would be a blow for barbarity and a victory for Penguanity. And as all the Emperors waddled off, they squawked in unison their own battlesquawk:

Penguanity! Penguanity! Penguanity!

\#

When the resident army was a hundred feet or so from the invading army, Plucky once again waddled to the front and gave them the same option as their fallen comrades had received: either lie down on your belly or die. And this time, surprisingly enough after being geed up by the battlesquawk of Penguanity, seven-hundred did exactly that, the other three hundred being quickly brought down by both harpoons and spears. The prostrate penguins were surrounded and told to get up. Terrified, they did as they were told. And now, to test their loyalty to the conquerors, these penguins were commanded to turn back and to round up all members of The Council and all of their toadies too. Round them up and put them in the cages. *They will be dealt with tomorrow.* And the penguins turned around and set off to do what they were told.

Meanwhile, hearing many a plaintive scream from female Emperors who were being attacked in their homes by Adélies, Plucky and One-Eye and the rest of the Emperors began going from igloo to igloo to put down those Adélies and to round up too any servants of the regime who were cowering in a hidden compartment. The Old King's jewellers' was broken into and the place was bare, not a single gold piece aglitter.

Though small compared to Emperor penguins, a thousand Adélies waddling amok were able to do a lot of damage in a few hours. After the last of them had been slaughtered, a headcount was made to comprehend this damage, and it was discovered that twenty-seven Emperor females had been killed, eight chicks had been killed, and too many of both had been raped and beaten overall.

#

The Food Wareigloo was a shambles and it would take weeks to clean it up and restock it. And the waddleways that crisscrossed the colony would need many, many flippers on deck to bring them back to their former glory. And whilst all these startling statistics were being taken into account, whilst anger was rising on seeing the death and destruction that these traitors from The Council had wrought upon their own penguins, their own species, still the Old King, The Chosen Penguin, was nowhere to be found. Neither he nor the rest of his brood.

And when they entered the peckles, what they saw turned the stomach of even the least squeamish of them: half-devoured chicks; vials of chickblood; all manner of little bloody knives and prods; cloacae encased in blocks of ice; a fertilized egg that had been severed in half, the chick's head in one half and its body in the other; and a skeleton, polished to a shine and hung above a sort of altar – and it was the skeleton of the penguin who had disappeared long ago after having asked the questions at a meeting about Penguanitarianism and forgiveness and if The Elders of Instinct could ever return.

CHAPTER 39: IN SEARCH OF KINGS

One-Eye and Plucky set out the next morning with a hundred penguins that were flippered to the beaks. Spears. Daggers. Harpoons. They arrived at the Old King's complex and there conversed with the securitypenguins. Where was he? Where was the scoundrel? Yes, they'd heard he had gone to the coast, but did he not come back? And then they noticed the footprints in the snow. Relatively fresh ones. And many of them too. Big ones and small ones. And before they began following these tracks, and though the others had pleaded for their lives, One-Eye gave the culling orders and the securitypenguins, their flippers trembling down by their sides and their heads hunched over their bodies, were killed – it was reasoned that anyone who could serve or protect such a parasitical and immoral penguin as the Old King was not one who could best serve the future needs of the colony. And when Plucky whispered to One-Eye that so many public killings might make more enemies than comrades here in the colony, One-Eye nodded in agreement but stated that the best way to flush out a potential enemy was by making him the enemy, and that much blood would still need to shed if the colony had any chance of regaining its original peace and harmony and overall prosperity.

      The footprints ended right before the shingle beach. And not knowing where to look from hereon in, One-Eye told them all to fan out. And if anyone was to see a King penguin, he was to squawk as loudly as he could and the rest would come tobogganing. They were to be captured if caught and nothing more. And as much as all wanted the King penguins to be killed as soon as possible, patience and reserve would be much in need: for these King penguins had to be executed publicly. A spectacle was needed to drive home the point to the other residents in the colony that The Chosen Penguin and all his progeny were not so special after all, and instead of being special they were just ordinary feathers and bones like any other.

CHAPTER 40: AS SLIPPERY AS AN EEL

Up on the glacier, the Old King was able to survey the movements all over the shingle beach. And he was able to survey the movements of Plucky, whom he recognized. And he was able to survey too that several of the party were beginning to approach the glacier. Whether they would bother scaling it or not was what he needed to know. And then, to his heart's despair, he saw them looking up towards him and nodding.

It would take them at least five minutes to get up to where he and his progeny were. And sensing that the jig was up, he began dictating to his sons and daughters and grandchicks what they would do. First and foremost, there was the crevice. Yes, a crevice that was just large enough to accommodate six chicks. What the Old King decided upon was law. If the chicks were chosen to be saved and no other, then they would be saved and the others would not. His sons nodded approval, somehow knowing that once that decision had been made, the rest of them could only hope for death, and a quick one at that.

But the Old King had another trick up his plumes. As he was unaware that the colony had been conquered, and as he presumed that those penguins down there had come from the sea, he made plans to get back to the colony and sound the alarm. All was not over yet, he proclaimed. Since the Emperor penguins, the fools that they were, were all scaling the glacier on the same side, the King penguins could give them the slip by tobogganing down the opposite side. And so, ensuring that enough food and freshwater and gold pieces and his own chunk of silver were in the crevice with the chicks, the Old King and his sons and daughters began covering the crevice with flipperfuls of compressed snow.

When the Emperor penguins got to the top of the glacier, there was nobody there. Had they listened carefully, they would have heard the nervous chirping of the chicks down in the covered-up crevice, but alas they themselves were too busily engaged in conversation and heard nothing. They stood there on the glacier for some time looking all about them, looking in all directions, and when about ten minutes had passed they noticed way down there, far off in a snowfield, a number of dark silhouettes waddling along. They could not tell if they were Emperors down there or Kings, but when they squinted their eyes and noticed the waddle movements, they knew that they were the latter. And then those silhouettes on reaching a slope took to tobogganing and disappeared down the other side. And so, the Emperors on the glacier began a great squawking, which was picked up by those Emperors who were still searching in between the rocks down there on the shingle beach. *King penguins ahoy! King penguins making a toboggan for it! Over yonder!*

And a mighty chase began.

CHAPTER 41: THE SIEGE ON THE GREENIE MONUMENT

The King penguins made it to the colony as darkness was descending. Together they crept along the lines of igloos. They were aware of the silhouettes standing outside the homes of the members of The Council, and overheard snippets of conversation regarding the next day's or the day after that's cull and how so many penguins had died and how the Adélies would not be causing the females and chicks any more problems from now on.

Some Emperors noticed the King penguins creeping along but thought due to their small size that they were just a few chicks who had been out playing and were now returning home a wee bit late. But a few Emperors did notice, even though there was not much light with which to see, that their waddle was not that of their own species.

#

The King penguins reached the Greenie Monument and flapped at the big doors. And after many long seconds, one of the doors opened slightly and a cleric's beak stuck out through the gap. And the cleric became much flustered when he realized just who these late callers were. And, not knowing what to do, he told the King penguins to wait there while he discussed the matter with the other clerics. Minutes passed. And the King penguins out there in the cold were beginning to be noticed by many eyes in the dark. And silhouettes were beginning to gather in number. And the sheen from several daggers was noticed too. And just when the King penguins thought they were done for, both double doors opened and they were ushered in, the doors slamming shut and bolted behind them.

#

There was much angst now in the Greenie Monument and the congregation was deadlocked between that of providing sanctuary to the King penguins and between that of turfing them out on their rear ends and leaving their destinies in the invaders' flippers. And much squawking and flapping ensued. And the clerics together had to squawk above the congregation's squawking and thereby try to restore some semblance of order.

It was given to the congregation that if they wished for the King penguins to be turfed out, The Chosen Penguins, the Old King himself being a medium through which He orchestrated no end of miracles, then they themselves were sinners and should leave the Order right now without wasting another second. The congregation suddenly fell silent. And then a sort of hissing took up, each penguin whispering to the next, one penguin nodding and the other nodding back. And then without further ado, half of the congregation got up from their bellies, unbolted the doors and waddled out.

To be sure, the clerics really had not expected this. In one fell swoop to lose half of their congregation spoke volumes of the stark reality that was closing in on them and the Order. Quite taken aback, the clerics cursed themselves for having issued such a curt ultimatum. Perhaps it could have been worded more diplomatically. But at the same time, the clerics felt that they were much indebted to The Chosen Penguin, he having given them gold in the past, he having even been behind many of their ordinations. Yes, the Old King had had his flippers in everything. And even though also he had undermined them and their Order many times over the seasons, he had become central to their belief system. And it was he who recovered The Sacred Greenstone that day on the shingle beach. And almost all Greenies believed, or had believed, that he was favoured by Him and that even his daughters' chicks, who were not present here now, had been brought into the world by Him, by The Greenmaker, and were thus semi-deities, semi-deities who could waddle on water as easily as waddling on ice.

Turning the Old King away now would undermine their entire Order and would do more damage than any icequake would if it were to shake the foundations of the Greenie Monument itself. No, by hell or high water, the King penguins would stay. And since the Greenie Monument was deemed hallowed ground, it was firmly believed that no blood could ever be shed herein since it was protected by The Greenmaker. Nobody or nothing could cross the threshold and cause violence. *And should those invaders barge in here and try to whisk away our beloved guests, The Chosen Penguins, we do not need to resist them whatsoever: for a simple Flipper of Greenliness will suffice in disarming any intruder, will suffice in melting the lump of ice in their chests into a warm beating heart.*

And no sooner had this been said than the double doors began to thud – the Emperor penguins outside were starting to ram it with a big chunk of driftwood. And every time the door shook, so too did the icy walls. And so too did the clerics and what remained of the congregation.

#

The ramming of the door ceased for a moment and the voice of One-Eye could be heard squawking up over the wall and down unto them. And One-Eye gave them the final ultimatum: flipper over the King penguins and all would be forgiven, forgiven since their Order was all about forgiveness at the end of the day; but should they continue to resist, there would be no future in the colony, either for them or their precious Order.

And now, the pressure really was on. And the halved congregation began squabbling once again, some of which tried to seize the Old King and drag him out to the invaders. And in an attempt to restore order, and knowing that it would mean a smaller congregation still, the clerics gave the same option yet again: *if you believe we should flipper over The Chosen Penguin and his progeny to the barbarians at the doors, then you too are a barbarian and the Order does not need your kind and it is best that we excommunicate you herefrom.*

All became silent. And then the hissing whispers started up and the heads began to nod at each other. And again, half of the halved congregation got up off their bellies, unbolted the doors and waddled out. But this time the doors were not bolted quickly enough and the invading Emperors swarmed in, brandishing their daggers and their spears, amongst which was Plucky. The congregants who waddled straight over to these invaders extended the Flipper of Greenliness to them but were either pushed to the side or had their flippers broken.

No blood shall ever be shed on this hallowed ground, proclaimed the clerics, angrily facing the invaders. *The Greenmaker knoweth all. And knoweth He who be good and who be evil. And smiteth he any barbarous intent in his Sacred Roofless Igloo.* And with that Plucky drove a dagger into the chest of one of the Old King's sons, who thereby fell to the ground and under whom a pool of crimson blood waxed large.

One-Eye entered thereafter and countered the preaching of the clerics by stating the following: *if one wishes to see and be one with The Greenmaker, he is free to yearn for that; however, let that be a private station. Henceforth, neither walls nor clerics shall be needed in this colony, as they were not needed long ago either. There will be no more assemblies. There will be no more highfalutin treachery either.*

And all dispersed therefrom. And the clerics were dragged out by their feathers and thrown into the cages. And the King penguins too. Except for the one whom Plucky stabbed and who had died. And except for the Old King, who was kept fettered in an igloo and for whom One-Eye kept an all-night vigil, lest he somehow escape or commit suicide. And although all King penguins were tortured throughout the night, not one of them would spill the beans on the whereabouts of the six chicks.

CHAPTER 42: EXPULSIONS! EXPULSIONS! & DEATH ROW!

There was much discussion amongst One-Eye and other old penguins as to what to do with the Greenie congregants, and the feminists too. In regard to the former, One-Eye himself had already confiscated The Sacred Greenstone from The Stonekeeper and had got a trusted youth to go to the cliffs and throw it into the sea.

Even though the Greenie congregants had been reduced in number, there were still too many to justify a cull without causing quite a stir, without causing possibly a revolt against them who had come to liberate the colony. And after many hours of back and forth, the wise old beaks decided that expulsion was the only measure that could satisfy all. Expulsion of all those who had been loyal and faithful to the Order until they had dragged their clerics away: for having them in the colony would always be a threat to the rest of the penguins, especially since they believed firmly in the King penguins being chosen above all other species.

And so, the following morning, the congregants would all get a knock on their door and be met by be-speared penguins who would give them each a week's supply of food and freshwater and tell them to sling their hook. And if they ever came back, they would be executed on the spot. No judge. No jury. Right there and then. Suffice it to say, though saddened by this command, not one single Greenie congregant would try to resist it. And the following morning too, a demolition crew would begin work on not only the peckles but on the walls of the Greenie Monument too, and by evening there would no longer be even a trace of either place.

In regard to the feminists, One-Eye and his kinspenguins had to move fast. Before the Greenie zealots had been expelled they made sure to get testimonies from them as to which of the feminists in the colony had thrown eggs at them – these feminists were then dragged out of their igloos and thrown into cages with the others. The other feminists, those who had not taken part in smashing eggs but had crowed over their rights to lay unfertilized eggs and who had repeated ad infinitum the progressive mantras taught to them by the Old King's daughters, well, these were all expelled on the same morning as the Greenies.

It was a droll sight to see both Greenies and feminists, enemies to the colony and to each other, to see both exiting at the same time. The Greenies waddled off to the right and the feminists to the left. But not long later, feeling cold and scared, the feminists doubled back and followed the Greenies' trail. On seeing this, Plucky wondered if the Greenies would take them in. Was not their creed all about forgiveness? Once one repented one was redeemed. And laughing to himself, Plucky bethought so many redemptions going on out there in the extreme cold the night to come.

#

As One-Eye did the rounds and spoke to those who had suffered so much under the old regime, it was brought to light that there had been a thriving porn industry, of which penguosexuality and chickophilia had been at the forefront. In fact, both sexualities which more times overlapped than not, had recently been decriminalized.

This angered the old penguin a great deal, as much as

when he had listened to the Old King's daughter over a week ago explain about the hatchery and unfertilized eggs, and how she had nonchalantly pointed out those five fertilized eggs with the splotch of red dye, those that had been marked out for life and destruction.

Although penguosexuality had existed for all time, it certainly had never been celebrated or facilitated in any way. It was looked upon as an aberration, an evolutionary cul-de-sac, and one that had to be eradicated as quickly as possible because anything that went against the colony and reproduction had to be eradicated. And that usually meant expulsion. And expulsion of an individual meant practically certain death: for when the blizzards hit, that individual would not have the huddle, that mass of bodies, to keep him warm.

But the crux of the matter lay in the fact that penguosexual penguins who had *come out of the icicle*, to use the progressive parlance, had, apart from the Old King himself, been very much involved in the sexualisation of chicks and grooming them so that they would join the prostitution game at such a tender young age. And as physically damaging on a chick's body as was rape by an Adélie penguin, rape by an Emperor penguosexual was usually death for the chick or, in a best case scenario, survival but with damaged organs and the guarantee of never being able to fertilize eggs. Obviously then, if it related to that other type of chickophile, which was rarer than the other, it meant the female chick victim, if she survived to adulthood, would never be able to lay eggs. And so massive had been this grooming scandal, so many penguosexuals involved, that One-Eye decided that expulsion just wouldn't be enough.

What was needed was justice for what they had done. And as a spectacle would be held for the culling of the members of The Council, the King penguins and all their Penguanitarian and Greenie cleric enablers, so too would the penguosexuals and egg-smashing feminists be added to that spectacle.

It was probable, the old penguins admitted when focusing in on the penguosexuals, that there were still several in the colony who were in the icicle as it were, and on witnessing this they would stay firmly in that icicle and not try to practice sodomy on either another consenting adult or a non-consenting chick.

CHAPTER 43: SOCIAL RE-ENGINEERING

As One-Eye stood before the rest of the Emperor penguins, he knew, instinctually he knew, that he only had a few days left to live. Soon the females, including his wife with whom he had bred every single season for two whole decades, would be here. And since there was much to be done and still much more to be said, he tried his best not to waste even a second of it, knowing that by not wasting any seconds would nonetheless accelerate his end. But for all that he held long meetings with Plucky and the bodybird and the old beaks and some new beaks too. And he advised them on what they had to do to safeguard the colony, to stop it from falling once again into a King penguin's flippers.

#

Culling was a prerequisite in order to have any healthy colony. The hardened criminal, One-Eye proclaimed, should never have the right to propagate his or her genes after having perpetrated an atrocity. And life in a cage for a criminal, though it be something, was a waste of the colony's resources withal.

#

And then they began to discuss the FQ – the Female Question. It was decided without much protraction that the fairer sex would no longer have rights bar that of laying eggs and looking after chicks and that of gathering and arranging nesting.

Yes, the Emperor penguin male had been the one, pre-fire, to look after the egg while the female hunted in the sea. And that had been fine and dandy, fine and natural back then. But the female's role in modern colony life would be different going forward. Given that she was the one who had waxed sentimental and broody when the Old King all those seasons ago had rocked up on the outskirts of their colony with his six chicks, she could not be trusted to make decisions, especially long-term decisions on the colony's overall welfare. It was female sentimentality and broodiness that had opened up the gates of hell.

And likewise, under such a malevolent influence as that of the King penguins, the females' natural broodiness and sentimentalism had easily been warped into that of unfertilized eggs and smashed fertilized eggs as well. No, the females would never again rule the roost. And likewise, it was postulated, if a female was always innocent, as she had been for the most part under the reign of the The Chosen Penguins, then she could not claim to have any autonomy whatsoever. Better that she retain her innocence so and lose her autonomy forever, it was agreed.

The conversations would then develop into that penguin species that was on the end of every Emperor's beak. And when pressed upon the fact, or what was thought of as a fact, that those Kings in the cages were the last King penguins in the world, One-Eye, though a very serious penguin, laughed. Indeed, he almost keeled over, so much was he in hysterics. When this laughter finally subsided, he was able to gather his thoughts and offer his response:

The last King penguins? Is that what the old rogue's been telling you? Why no doubt there are more King penguins out there in the world than there are Emperors. And no doubt, more will come in the years ahead with their flippers out for food and water whilst at the same time their beaks will squawk about genocide in some far-flung place, the atrocity committed by some little-known or unknown species. And all the time he'll be squawking and crying and wailing, his beady black eyes will be roving over all that you possess, roving covetously over all you and your forefathers have built up. No better demolition expert is there out there than the King penguin. But instead of destroying buildings, he destroys the social weal. He destroys trust. He destroys Nature Herself. He is a parasite. Whether you hearken the ancient legends of his trickery or you hearken scientific spiels on primordial soups, he is, without a shadow of a doubt, the immortal parasite. And a parasite is only ever as strong as the host is weak. And henceforth we Emperor penguins in this colony must not be weak. We must do the moral thing for our species. And if by doing the moral thing for our species means that it is immoral for another species, well then, that is not our concern. Our sole concern is for our species and for no other. Our quest here is a simple one. To be hatched. To grow. To reproduce. And to die. And if along the way, we can think about things, if along the way we can get pleasure from simple things, things such as the hidden wonders from the seas or listening to a raconteur around the fire or the act of reproduction or the tender peck from one's monogamous partner or gazing with delight and curiosity at the night sky without getting too highfalutin and dogmatic, then all the better.

CHAPTER 44: THE GREAT CULL

The day of the cull came. Many expected the guilty ones to be hanged. But One-Eye, ever wise and ever thinking of how to hit two birds with the one stone, had in mind a culling style that though somewhat unorthodox would be second to none and offer the colony a clean break from all enemies, from all feathered threats.

#

To a snowfield a mile outside the colony the prisoners were brought. And there in the middle of the snowfield were they manacled and fettered once again and left lying supinely. Immobile now, there could be no struggle. The only struggle could be that of the voice. And though their collective squawks and brays would be shrill and piercing for ages, so too would that end. And end in a gruesome but wholly natural way.

The cull did not have a set time. Whether very old or very young or very squeamish, it mattered not: all the residents of the colony were forced to attend, forced to witness the oncoming and bloody event. And they were told to form a circle and to keep that circle back some distance from the hundred or so prisoners, of whom were the King penguins, the members of the Council, Penguanitarian and Greenie cleric enablers of the regime, feminists and penguosexuals/chickophiles.

At the front of this encirclement were many Emperors with spears. And not knowing exactly what was going to happen here, the audience thought these Emperors would cull the prisoners by spearing them. Hours passed by. And nothing seemed to happen. And the audience became restless. They could not leave however. And the squawks and brays from the tied-up prisoners died down due to hoarseness or tedium.

And then, seemingly out of nowhere, did a single skua alight on the snow twenty or so feet from one of the prisoners, who happened to be a member of The Council. The skua hopped closer and then hopped back. It was as if the bird were testing the reflexes of the member of The Council. And after hopping back, it noticed that there had been no movement from the member of The Council. And learning from this, the skua hopped forward four times in a row and stopped. Again, there was no movement from the member of The Council. And taking this into account, the skua hopped onto the chest of the member of The Council and began pecking at his eyes.

Never had any Emperor heard such a shrill sound as that which came out of that prisoner's beak. Peck, peck, peck, went the skua. And scream, scream, scream, went the prisoner. And his scream made the other prisoners scream with him. And these screams that filled the air must have sounded like a dinner bell for the other skuas because suddenly there was a whole flock of them, maybe as many as forty, and they were all alighting on the chests of the prisoners. And the screaming went up another few decibels, the sound amplified by the cold moist air and the snow. And the snow began to turn red. And thereafter did it turn pink and slushy.

It was noticed and considered somewhat peculiar that two of prisoners, two Greenie clerics, did not pray or shout out to The Greenmaker as they were being devoured alive. And in the centre of all these prisoners was the Old King. And still there was no skua on his chest pecking at his eyes or trying to rip open up his belly. And when the collective screaming reached its climax, the anti-climax was incredibly swift, a silence falling over the pink snowfield of still bodies or ones that were trembling merely from raw and exposed nerves.

But the largest of the skuas, having torn a penguosexual

to pieces and having devoured half of his carcass, seemed to look over at the Old King and to have recognized him, whereupon he leapt off the penguosexual's carcass and onto the Old King's chest. But he did not immediately start pecking at the black beady eyes. He seemed to be conversing with him in the Skuaish language. And the Old King spoke to him in as jovial a manner as he could, given the circumstances. And he told the big skua that if he pecked at his manacles and fetters, he could set him free. And if he set him free, he would reward him with a season's supply of eggs, fertilized or unfertilized, whichever he preferred, and chicks too, he could get him chicks too, nice chubby and meaty chicks.

The big skua, however, was not one for stifling his need for instant gratification. The big skua could only sense the warm body beneath of the King penguin his feet and smell the warm rivulets of blood that babbled therein. He could not put off the bounty of now for a future one. His brain could not even register that abstract season of abstract eggs and abstract chicks. And his response to the Old King's offer was not one by way of a squawk but rather through one massive peck right through the left eye, which sent the Old King's body shivering all over. And a few pecks thence did that body cease shivering and become as still as all the others.

#

The residents did not cheer once the Old King had been culled, though many of them celebrated his demise inwardly with glee, as they had celebrated with glee all the other prisoners and how they had all died in a similar way, a traumatic and torturous way. But even now the culling was not at an end.

The audience was told not to leave but to stay put because more was to come. And so they waited. But what they were waiting for now was a mystery to them. The prisoners were all dead after all. What more could be expected? And they watched the skuas continuing to feast on all the carcasses.

And one by one, the skuas became satiated and sat down in the snow, unable to move from such gluttony. And when the last skua, the big one who had devoured half the carcass of the penguosexual and most of the carcass of the Old King, yes, when he sat down in the snow, One-Eye let out a thunderous bray, and Plucky and a score of other Emperor penguins with spears came in from all angles and set upon the skuas. And this spectacle lasted less than two minutes, the spears flying true, the skuas unable to fly or make much of a dash for it over the pink snow, and those that got as far as the audience were speared by other Emperors. And when this act had finished, the Emperors with the spears waddled back to the circle. And now it could be seen that the slain skuas were in a heap with the carcasses of the prisoners.

And as he would die in his sleep by the open fire that night, what happened next was One-Eye's final public act. He waddled over to the heap of carcasses with a lit length of driftwood. And accompanying him were four young penguins who carried bags of oil, bags fashioned from seal stomachs and which were stretched almost to ripping due to the heavy volume within. And the bags were placed atop the heap and within the heap and around the heap. And only then did One-Eye reach the lit length of driftwood into the centre of the heap and thereby set it all alight.

A great tongue of flame went up and the audience applauded the sight. And as all the carcasses became engulfed, it seemed that one was moving of its own accord. And this was pointed out by a few penguins in the audience. But when they looked more closely at it, they reassured themselves that it had been an optical illusion, the movement of the flame being mistaken for the movement of a body. And when the applause died down, One-Eye pointed his flipper at Plucky as a sign for him to join him at the bonfire. And another applause rang out across the pink snowfield. And when Plucky reached One-Eye, the latter got down onto the snow in a prostate position, a sign that his short leadership was now being relinquished and flippered over to Plucky.

CHAPTER 45: NAME THE KING! & CLOSE ONE-EYE

And that night, before dozing off to death, One-Eye had sent a messenger to bring Plucky and the bodybird to him. And Plucky, who had been busily engaged in a meeting with the netters over plans to get food and food distribution back on track, dropped everything and came tobogganing to the open fire. The bodybird, who had been mending the soldiers' broken flippers from the battle, did likewise.

And what One-Eye had to say to them was about the King penguin. Though his squawks were now weak and barely audible, he was able to leave Plucky and the bodybird with his final pearls of wisdom.

The plague that was the King penguin was no more for their colony. But complacency setting in would always be a threat. And increased complacency came from increased technological innovations and the convenience that was derived therefrom. And so, the Emperors could not rest assured that he would never come back to Antarctica because he would, as surely as night follows day and day night. He would be back. *They* would be back. Someday.

And for starters, as a way to remind themselves of this constant threat, the Emperors were to etch the memory of the King penguin's tyranny into the hearts and minds of the average Emperor penguin. And for this, One-Eye suggested they etch the nefariousness of the King penguin as a viral a disease into the very landscape itself. And this would be done by placing names on certain snowfields and beaches and glaciers.

Henceforth, for example, the snowfield in which all had been executed would now be known as *Kingblood Snowfield*. A glacier yonder that could be gazed upon from any part of the colony would henceforth be known as *Killking Glacier*. And the shingle beach whence many young Emperor males had set off on a wild goose chase to save fictitious King penguins would hereon in and forever be known as *Kingtrick Beach*. And furthermore, large stones would be set up high on the cliffs over that beach, four-hundred-and-ninety-nine to be exact, one for each of the penguins who had lost his life in that madness. And other landmarks were mentioned and renamed, all bearing a connection to the King penguin and his parasitism and treachery and greed.

And so, brayed One-Eye, once colony life had been restored to its former glory, once all had food in their bellies and a roof over their heads and a warm hearth and a monogamous partner and eggs, many, many eggs and chicks, once the population had been restored too, then, One-Eye stated, the squawk breaking off now and then mid-sentence, well, then, the Emperors were to begin expeditions.

And these expeditions would probably be one-way trips. They would be, in a word, blood sacrifices: for neither colony nor species could survive without a blood sacrifice ever generation – it was the way of things and had always been the way of things, though recently forgotten under the cudgels of convenience and materialism. And these expeditions were to be carried out so as to search for King penguins. Seek and cull. Seek and cull.

For as long as there were King penguins in the world, no Emperor penguin could ever plan for a more prosperous future because the cycle would constantly be broken down into terror and exploitation and degeneracy by the King. And though the forefathers of the Emperors had failed in this going by the ancient legends, and though he himself, although he had protested with the other Elders of Instinct and lost an eye and his colony residency for those protests, he too had failed. And so, it befell the likes of Plucky and the bodybird, and the Emperor penguins that would come long after both of them, to go out into the blue yonder, to go to the other end of the world if need be, and to search out the King. *To seek and to cull*, One-Eye repeated before his head began to nod and he drifted off to sleep. And straddling the line between wakefulness and sleep, his beak opened and lightly repeated the mantra:

To seek and to cull.

CHAPTER 46: DARWIN'S NATURAL SELECTION

The marine iguanas from the rocks watched with trepidation a chunk of ice bobbing past them whereupon stood six King penguins. And the six King penguins had recently moulted and lost their brown downy feathers. They had become adults. And etched into the ice was gold, lots and lots of gold. And even though the iceberg was only ten percent in size to what it had been when it first snapped off Antarctica, there was still ample room for the King penguins to waddle about thereon.

And the iceberg or what remained of it was pushed by the current up onto a beach, whereupon the King penguins hopped off of it and quickly began to peck out from it their pieces of gold. And one King penguin, the son of one of the daughters and the son or grandchick of the Old King himself, had a striking resemblance to the latter, especially the way he waddled, and more especially the way he covetously took in his surroundings with those black beady eyes.

And when all the gold had been transported up beyond the tidal zone of the beach and hidden, and a lump of silver too, the King penguins waddled along the coast in search of something. A giant tortoise saw them and turned and shuffled off in the opposite direction. And two miles hence did the Kings encounter a small colony of Galapagos penguins. And strangely, very strangely, were they able to converse quite fluently with those local penguins.

And the local penguins informed them that they were an endangered species, that the Galapagos penguin had less specimens than any other species of penguin. And no sooner had the Galapagos penguins said this than the King penguins began a great wailing and squawking and crying and tearing plumage straight out of their chests. And this great scene of hysterics unnerved the Galapagos penguins who asked them why they were so sad, why they appeared so woebegone.

And to this, still wailing and flapping and crying, the King penguins filled them in on events: how they were even more endangered a species than were the Galapagos penguins since they had escaped from a bloodbath, a massacre, a genocide, a cull, all the other King penguins being murdered on Antarctica by those dastardly and evil Emperor penguins; how thanks to whatever god or gods or abstract concept the Galapagos penguins believed in, the King penguins were able to survive against the odds; and it was not the current that had brought them hither but rather destiny. Yes, the Galapagos penguins' god or gods or abstract concept had brought them here to help them, to help the Galapagos penguins, to introduce them to gold and how trading in gold would put their colony firmly on the road to Progress and Nurture. And not alone that, but they would also gift them with that warm and fuzzy ideology called Penguanitarianism.

And what, the Galapagos penguins asked, quite mystified but intrigued at the same time, *what exactly is Penguanitarianism?*

And the six King penguins began to squawk in unison, each word coming from each beak simultaneously as though rehearsed for a great piece of drama that would soon take place and be realer, so much realer, than life itself.

Printed in Great Britain
by Amazon